O'Grady threw open the office door and brought up his rifle. Jessie stepped to his side and pushed the gun's muzzle down. He said, "Now's the time to hit them, Jessie! Before Goodwin can get those rifles handed out!"

"Wait, Tim," Jessie told him. "Give Ki a chance."

As they watched, Ki slid a handful of star-shaped blades from a leather pouch and began to throw...

— WESLEY ELLIS —

LONE STAR
AND THE
MONTANA TROUBLES

A JOVE BOOK

LONE STAR AND THE MONTANA TROUBLES

A Jove book/published by arrangement with
the author

PRINTING HISTORY
Jove edition/August 1984

ISBN: 0-515-07748-8

Jove books are published by The Berkley Publishing Group,
200 Madison Avenue, New York, N.Y. 10016. The words
"A JOVE BOOK" and the "J" with sunburst are trademarks
belonging to Jove Publications, Inc.

Chapter 1

This time the attack was planned to be launched suddenly, in the dark hours before daybreak. If the cartel's raiders had not made a mistake in the darkness and cut the Circle Star's eastern perimeter fence within earshot of a line shack, the raid could have caught those in the main house while they slept.

Cottontop Barnes awoke in the shack when the first tight-stretched strand of barbwire twanged as it was severed by the nippers. Like most cowhands passing the night in a line shack, Barnes had been sleeping lightly and fully clothed except for his boots and wide-brimmed Stetson.

His first thought was that he'd been roused by the harsh, metallic-sounding shriek of a desert nighthawk. Then the second strand of barbwire sang as the nippers parted it, and Cottontop knew at once what was happening. He was into his boots and standing in the line shack's door, peering through the moonless darkness, when the third and final strand was cut. Then a man's gruff voice reached his ears.

"All right, you men. Before we go any further, wrap them tow sacks around your horses' hooves. And be damn sure you get 'em tied on tight! I don't want none of your nags to trip up and raise a ruckus when we get close to where we're heading."

"I don't see why we got to handle this damn job when it's so dark a man can't see his hand out in front of his nose," another man said, his voice grouchy.

"We got a ways to go yet," the first man replied. "It'll be light enough to shoot by when we get there."

"Me, I still think we'll do one hell of a lot better if we wait till daylight," the complainer grumbled. "It beats me why we got to—"

"We're doing the job when the boss told us to do it, that's why!" the man who'd spoken first broke in. "And you ain't gettin' paid for thinking, but because you're supposed to be able to hit what you're aiming at when you pull a trigger! Now shut up and get busy with them sacks. We don't want nobody to hear us till we're in easy range."

Barnes's saddle was lying just inside the door of the shack. He got it out quickly, moving as silently as possible, and began saddling up. He was ready to ride before the intruders moved, but waited until he heard the muffled hoofbeats of the gang moving onto Circle Star range. Even before the hushed thudding died away, he was in the saddle and anxious to move, but as a precaution he gave the nightriders a few minutes to get out of earshot, then started on a circuitous course for the Circle Star headquarters.

Cottontop had an advantage over the midnight raiders. He knew exactly where the main house was, and while the invaders were moving slowly, Barnes made a beeline ride. He kicked his horse to a gallop as soon as he figured he'd put enough distance between himself and the raiders, counting on the noise they made to cover the hoofbeats of his own cow pony. He figured that he was a good ten or fifteen minutes ahead of them when he reined in at the Circle Star bunkhouse.

Jessie stirred in her sleep when she heard Barnes galloping up, then awoke when the hoofbeats stopped. She could think of no reason why anyone should be arriving at the Circle Star in such a hurry at such an ungodly hour, but experience had long since taught her that it could mean nothing but trouble. She looked out her window and saw the shadowy form of horse and rider at the bunkhouse. Without lighting a lamp, she reached for her clothing.

Ki, in his own bedroom down the hall, awoke fully and at once. He stepped to the window and peered into the gloom. Even in the moonless blackness, he recognized Barnes by the way he moved as the line rider swung out of his saddle in front of the bunkhouse. Like Jessie, Ki knew that only trouble could have brought Barnes in from his job. Putting on his loose-fitting shirt and his jeans, Ki slid his feet into his rope-soled cotton slippers, then went to rouse Jessie.

"I'm up," Jessie called when Ki tapped softly on her door. "Wait just a minute, and we'll walk over to the bunkhouse together and see what's wrong."

When she emerged from her room a moment later, she had on the cowboy-style clothing she was accustomed to wearing when at home on Circle Star land. A flat-crowned tan Stetson sat squarely atop her thick, coppery blond hair, which spilled down across the shoulders of a cotton plaid shirt. A pair of denim trousers hugged the classic contours of her slender, muscular hips and thighs, and were tucked into the tops of a pair of well-kept range boots. She buckled on her gunbelt with its .38 Colt as she and Ki went down the stairs, then took a waist-length denim jacket from a wall peg next to the front door, to ward off the early-morning chill. From a glass-fronted gun case she removed her Winchester carbine.

As she checked the rifle's load, Ki debated briefly with himself as to whether he also should take a rifle, but decided against it; he normally shunned firearms in favor of his own personal and quite adequate arsenal. At the moment his weaponry consisted of an array of small throwing blades— *shuriken*—that he carried in the many pockets of his well-

3

worn black leather vest, as well as the delicately curved short *tanto* knife in its lacquered sheath, tucked into the waistband of his jeans. He rarely needed more than these.

Satisfied with the readiness of her rifle, Jessie nodded to Ki and they left the main house and strode toward the group of Circle Star hands standing in a group in front of the bunkhouse.

"How many you think there was, Cotton?" Ed Wright was asking Barnes as Jessie and Ki came up.

"Sounded like a dozen, but they might be as many as twenty," Barnes told the foreman. "It was too dark to rightly count 'em, and that's as close as I can come to guessing, after they put muffles on their nags' hooves."

"Rustlers?" one of the men asked from the darkness.

"I'd imagine," Wright replied. "There's that herd on the south range, it'd likely be the one they're after."

"I didn't finish telling you what they said, Ed," Barnes objected. "They wasn't talking 'bout steers. Whoever's bossing this deal told 'em they had to get near enough to shoot good. In my book, that means they're coming right here, to the main house. Near as I was to 'em, I didn't make no mistake 'bout what I heard, you can button a cow's tail on me if I'm wrong."

Before Wright could speak, Jessie said thoughtfully, "You told me yesterday that outside of that herd on the south section, all the other big herds are on the west range, Ed. And it's not likely there'd be a dozen or more men in a party of rustlers."

"Jessie's got a point, Ed," Ki agreed. "Rustlers don't usually travel in a gang that size."

Jessie added, "If they're rustlers and didn't head for the south, they'd have come in from the west, where the other big herds are. Besides—" She fell silent, thinking of the broken terrain in the northeastern part of the sprawling Circle

4

Star. She would never forget that it was in that cut-up area of narrow ridges and shallow canyons where the cartel's raiders had struck when they ambushed and murdered her father.

Ki knew her unspoken thought at once. "Jessie's right, Ed," he told the foreman. "That bunch isn't after cattle, they're after her."

"One of you men step in the bunkhouse and douse that lamp," Wright said instantly. "Ki figures to be right. You men mount up fast. If we play our hand cagey, we got a chance to surprise them murdering scoundrels."

Jessie and Ki had already started for the small corral where Sun, her palomino, was kept. Ki had no favorite mount, but used whichever of the cow ponies was handiest. To keep Sun company, there was always a horse or two in the corral with the magnificent animal. They saddled quickly.

"Do you want to take over from Ed?" Jessie asked as they worked.

"No," Ki replied. "Ed and I understand each other. He's the foreman, but if I suggest something to him, he'll do it."

"Are you going to give him an idea of what to do, then?"

"Yes, of course. Ed's a fine foreman when it comes to handling men and cattle, but his mind's not tuned to fighting until after the first shots are fired. If we have time, we might be able to trap those nightriders."

"It's the cartel," Jessie said as she cinched the last saddle strap on Sun and stood waiting for Ki to finish getting his horse ready.

He nodded and said, "They've left us in peace here at the Circle Star longer than usual. We should have been looking for trouble of some kind."

Only a few of the men had finished saddling and returned from the main corral when Jessie and Ki returned to the bunkhouse, leading their horses. Ed Wright was among them. He said to Jessie, "I know there ain't any use in me saying this, Jessie, but don't you think you better stay here to keep an eye on things? I'm leaving Cookie—he's getting a pot of coffee on and fixing breakfast for us when we get back."

"You're right. I have no intention of staying here," Jessie answered. "I'll be more at home with you and the men than I would be in the kitchen, anyhow. We'll ride whenever you give the word, Ed."

Ki said quickly, "You're going to split our men, aren't you, Ed? Try to catch the nightriders in a crossfire?"

After a moment of hesitation, Wright replied, "Something like that, Ki. Soon as all of 'em get here, we'll divide up."

Jessie nodded. "That sounds good to me. Put Ki and me where we're needed, and let's move off."

With Jessie and Ki heading one group and Wright the other, the Circle Star hands divided into two parties as soon as they left the main house. They did not try to move fast, but kept their mounts on a tight rein, listening for the sounds of riders approaching and trying to probe the darkness ahead of them.

Their caution earned a quick reward. They'd been advancing for only a few careful minutes when the muffled hoofbeats of the nightriders sounded ahead of them. Ki and Jessie reined in, and the half-dozen Circle Star hands behind them pulled up as well.

"Keep your shots a little to our left," Ki said quietly. "Ed and his bunch are off to our right somewhere close, so don't risk hitting any of our own men."

Jessie fired the first shot, and with its whiplike crack the others joined her. Wild cries of surprise shattered the blackness ahead, drowned by the crackling of rifle fire from the group under Wright's command. The Circle Star defenders got off a second volley before the invaders returned the fire. Red flame spurted from the rifles of the intruders, but it was a scattered effort. Slugs whistled menacingly to the left and right of the Circle Star hands, but all went wild, none of the hot lead coming anywhere close. Meanwhile, the muzzle flashes from the raiders' rifles gave the ready guns of the Circle Star hands a quick fix on their target area.

"One more round and move up on them!" Jessie commanded.

With a quick fusillade the Circle Star men responded, then spurred ahead in spite of the scattered return fire they got from the intruders. They squinted, trying to see through the darkness, but were unable to find targets.

When they heard Wright's bunch fire again, they were watching for the return fire from the raiders. Without waiting for further orders from Jessie or Ki, they began shooting toward the place where they'd last seen the muzzle blasts. A man yelled hoarsely, and a horse neighed. The men were firing at random now, since they'd seen no muzzle blasts.

"Hold your fire!" Ki called. "You're wasting shots!"

They waited, rifles poised, but no more gunfire came from the blackness. In the dead silence, the muted thudding of hoofbeats could be heard fading in the distance.

One of the men exclaimed, "Looks to me like the sons of—" He stopped, remembering that Jessie was present, and amended his words, finishing, "Like the sons of guns has turned tail and run. Are we going after 'em?"

"No," Jessie said quickly. Then she raised her voice to call out, "Ed!"

From the darkness, Wright replied, "I hear you, Jessie!"

"Don't chase after them, Ed!" Jessie went on. "They're not going to stop until their horses are ready to founder, and we don't have much chance of trailing them in the darkness!"

7

"That's good enough for me!" Wright called. "We'll turn back, then!"

Guided toward each other by hoofbeats a few minutes after they'd started their return, the two groups soon met and merged. Jessie nudged Sun ahead with the toe of her boot and joined Ed Wright at the head of the group. They rode side by side in silence for a few minutes before either of them spoke.

"I've sent a couple of boys back to the line shack with Cottontop," Wright told Jessie. "They'll stand watch and mend the fence at the same time. They oughta have the job done by daylight."

"That won't be too long, either," Jessie said, looking back to the east, where a faint trace of gray was beginning to spread along the horizon.

"I sorta figured it was getting close to daybreak, the way my stomach commenced acting up," Wright replied. "And instead of putting the hands to working cattle today, I think I'd best send 'em out two by two, on patrol. I'll tell 'em to ride all the boundary fences and make sure everything's all right. From today on, I'll have two hands in them line shacks along the east fence line, in case that gang decides to come back and try someplace else."

"That's fine, Ed," Jessie said. "And later today, or maybe tomorrow, you might let the hands know there'll be something extra in their pay at the end of the month. Just my way of thanking them for turning out ready to fight the way they did."

"Now you know they don't expect nothing extra, Jessie," Wright said.

"I know it. But I feel like they've earned something."

"Well, I don't suppose there's a man of 'em that can't use a few dollars extra, but the way I was brought up, when

8

you ride for a brand, fighting for it goes along with the job."

After they'd ridden on for a short distance in silence, the foreman asked, "What do you think that bunch was after this time, Jessie?"

"Oh, I'm sure Ki and I were their targets, as usual. And they wanted to do as much damage as they could, if they didn't have a chance at us." Jessie spoke calmly, almost casually. "If you'll think back, the cartel raids the Circle Star at least once a year, and sometimes twice, whether they have a reason to or not."

"Hoping they'll get lucky one of them times, I guess," Ed said.

"Something like that," Jessie agreed. She gestured ahead, toward the rectangle of light that showed through the cook-house windows. "It looks like Cookie's ready for us. I think Ki and I will join you for breakfast, Ed. It's been a busy morning already, and it's not even daylight yet."

After breakfast, in Alex Starbuck's study—at least, Jessie still thought of the big room that way—Ki repeated the question Ed Wright had asked her as they were riding back.

"Why, Jessie?" His black, almond-shaped eyes regarded her with unspoken concern. "What reason could the cartel have for raiding us right at this time?"

"I've been wondering about that myself, Ki," Jessie said. She was sitting in the big leather armchair that had been Alex's favorite, her cheek resting on its high back, which still retained a hauntingly faint fragrance of the cherry-flavored pipe tobacco her father had favored. "And I think I might see a reason, even if it does seem a little far-fetched."

"If you've got a reason, I'd like to hear it."

Ki sat down on the long, low divan that stood at an angle

9

in front of the fireplace and looked at Jessie, a thoughtful frown furrowing his brow. He was well aware that she did her clearest thinking in the study, and he believed this was due to her father's lingering presence here, even long after his death. Ki didn't believe in ghosts, but the Japanese part of him accepted the idea of *kime,* the life-spirit that lingers well past the death of the body, and can be felt by those who were closest to the deceased.

"Think back over the last three or four times the cartel's sent its nightriders to attack us, Ki," Jessie said.

"Well, they attacked when young Bobby Tinker came looking for us, to get help for his grandfather," Ki said thoughtfully. "But I don't count that, because they were trailing the boy. And before that—"

"Before that," Jessie broke in when Ki stopped while he searched his memory, "before that, they tried to stop us in San Antonio, when we were on the way to Outlaw Mountain. And another time, just before we started out to move against the land grabbers in California. And—well, I'm sure if we thought back a bit, we'd find that when the cartel is getting ready to try and wreck some Starbuck enterprise, they sometimes stage an attack on the Circle Star just to divert our attention."

Ki said slowly, "You know, Jessie, it had never occurred to me before to connect those raids on the Circle Star with what the cartel might be trying to do somewhere else. But now that you've mentioned it, there has been a connection more than once."

"I think so," Jessie replied. "And I'm surprised that I haven't seen it before. Or maybe I just had a hunch, and didn't pay enough attention to it."

"I think you're right," Ki told her, standing up to stretch and flex his muscles. "But I can't think of a thing going on

10

in any of the Starbuck businesses right now that you'd need to be concerned about."

"Neither can I," Jessie said. "And that bothers me. If my hunch is right, there may be something going on that we haven't heard about yet. But tomorrow's mail day, and maybe we'll get a clue of some kind then."

It was late the following afternoon when the young cowhand sent by Ed Wright to pick up the mail at the flagstop station on the Southern Pacific returned with a bulging saddlebag. Jessie sorted the mail, and because Ki had ridden off with the men after breakfast to check on the south range, she walked over to the bunkhouse with the half-dozen letters and postcards addressed to the hands, and gave them to the cook to be distributed when the men returned for supper. Then she went back to the house, took the mail that remained on the long library table in the living room, and retired to the study.

Because the business and industrial empire created by Alex Starbuck spanned the continent and extended to Europe and the Far East, there were few mail deliveries that did not contain a half-dozen or more oversized manila envelopes.

These, Jessie knew, contained thick sheaves of reports on the condition of various Starbuck holdings. She looked at the bulging envelopes and was thankful that not all the businesses made their reports at the same time. She imagined herself trying to cope with a single mail delivery with reports from banks and real-estate operations in New York and San Francisco; a brokerage house with branches in Paris, Rome, London, Boston, and Chicago; timber and lumber operations in Michigan and the Pacific Northwest; copper mines in Montana, coal mines and gold mines in Colorado; a steel

11

mill in Pennsylvania and another in Illinois; plantations in Hawaii; and the import-export house that had been Alex's first business, and which still flourished in Tokyo, Hong Kong, and San Francisco.

Quickly Jessie pushed away the business mail and looked at the tiny heap of personal correspondence that remained. One of the letters caught her attention at once. Not only was its envelope creased and stained, but she did not recognize the handwriting, and the letter was addressed not to her, but to Alex.

Slitting the envelope open, Jessie read the short letter quickly. A puzzled expression grew on her face as she scanned the scrawled lines. By the time she'd finished reading the letter, the puzzled look had become a thoughtful frown. She put the letter aside and shuffled through the big manila envelopes until she'd found one she remembered. Opening it, she began studying the pages of figures it contained.

Not satisfied with what she'd seen, Jessie went to the battered rolltop desk and took a file folder from its oversized bottom drawer. She was still going through the pages she'd selected from the folder when Ki came in.

He saw the expression on Jessie's face, and asked, "What's wrong?"

"I'm not sure anything's exactly wrong," she replied slowly. "But it just may be that I've stumbled on the next place the cartel's going to attack."

For a moment Ki stared at Jessie, puzzled. "What do you mean, Jessie, you *may* have discovered where we can look for trouble next? Aren't you sure?"

Jessie shook her head. "No. Not at all."

"Maybe you'd better explain," he suggested.

"Ki, you remember what we were talking about the other night? How the cartel seems to signal that they're going to make a major move against us somewhere else by staging an attack here on the Circle Star?"

"Of course I remember. But we decided we didn't have any way to find out where they were going to make their real attack."

"I think I've found a clue, but I may be wrong. I'd like to know whether you agree with me, or whether I'm just letting my imagination run wild."

"You've never worried about imagining things before," Ki said. "And it isn't like you to be unsure of yourself."

"It's not myself I'm unsure of," Jessie said wryly. "I'm just not convinced that I'm on solid ground. I feel like I might be trying to catch a handful of wind."

"Tell me about your hunch," he suggested.

"First read this letter," she said, passing him the single scrawled sheet that had been in the envelope addressed to her father.

Ki read the few lines aloud: "'Mr. Starbuck—I don't want to lose the nice house you fixed for us all in Starhope, but there's bad things happening at your mine, and that's what could happen unless you stop it. Please do.'"

Looking up from the letter, Ki said, "It isn't signed, Jessie. And I can see why you're confused about its meaning, because it really doesn't make much sense. You're sure the letter came from Starhope?"

"Of course I am." She passed Ki the envelope, pointing to the postmark. "If you've forgotten, the Post Office Department decided to give both Starbuck and Anaconda our own postmarks."

"Of course. The Copperopolis post office was being swamped with our mail," Ki said. "That was a long time ago, and it had slipped my mind. The Anaconda just used their name, but Alex didn't want his name to be used on a postmark, so he suggested they use Starhope instead."

"That's right. Besides, he said it would make the people living in Starhope feel more like the town was real."

Ki looked at the envelope again and said, "This letter must have gone out through the office at the mine. But how could anybody in Starhope not know that Alex is dead?"

"That's one of the things that confuses me," Jessie said. "The other is how someone could have gotten a letter addressed to Alex stamped with the Starhope postmark. All the outgoing mail is handled by the office at the mine, and surely somebody would have noticed how the envelope was addressed."

Ki shook his head. "Not necessarily. Stamping envelopes is a pretty boring job. More than likely the clerk handling the mail the day this went out wasn't looking at the addresses on the envelopes, but just sat there stamping the postmark."

Jessie nodded. "It could've happened that way."

"You said you thought you'd figured out where the cartel is going to attack us next," Ki said after a moment's silence. "You mean the Starbuck copper mines, of course?"

"Yes."

"This letter's a pretty flimsy thing to—"

Jessie interrupted him. "It's not just the letter, Ki."

"What else, then?"

"After I'd thought about the letter and the way it ties in with what we were talking about, the way the cartel moves, I looked at the mine's operating statement for the past month. It came in today's mail too. And it doesn't look right, Ki. I got out the statements for the past several months, and they don't look right, either."

"I guess I don't follow you, Jessie. What doesn't look right about them?"

"Ki, ever since Alex bought those copper mines, they've produced just about the same amount of ore every month, and the ore's yielded about the same amount of copper.

14

Well, ore production hasn't changed, but the copper yield has dropped consistently."

"Couldn't the mines be producing lower-grade ore?"

Jessie shook her head. "No. If the ore was lower grade, the amount of silver would be lower too. It's not."

"How did you find out about all this, Jessie?"

"I haven't really found out anything positive, Ki. You see, the assay reports for the past four months are missing from the statements. They do show the amount of money received from the sale of copper and silver, though. That's where I noticed that we've been getting the same amount of money from silver, but not nearly as much for copper."

"And silver's just a by-product, of course," Ki commented.

"Yes. There's so little silver in a ton of copper that it's not really very important. But if the amount of copper the mines produce goes down, the amount of silver should go down too."

"I see what you're getting at," Ki said. "And the letter addressed to Alex might have been referring to the skullduggery you suspect is going on at the mine."

"I certainly don't think it's just a coincidence."

"So we're going to Montana, where you can find out for yourself what's happening?"

"I think we have to, Ki. That letter from Starhope and the figures on those reports need to be looked into. Because if you take them together, they could be the signal that the copper mines will be the next place where the cartel is planning to attack us."

Chapter 2

Jessie and Ki stood on the platform of the Sarah, Texas, railroad station, waiting for the westbound train. Both of them had given up the customary garb they wore around the Circle Star, and were now clad in less conspicuous clothing—Ki in a dark suit, low-topped Wellington boots, and a wide-brimmed black hat, Jessie in a green wool traveling suit with a flowing skirt and a form-fitting jacket, her coppery hair gathered in a conservative roll at the back of her neck.

The town of Sarah had been built by Jessie's father as a living memorial to his wife, Jessie's mother, and so it bore her name. She had been an early casualty of the cartel's ruthless war against the Starbuck interests, and her death had begun a series of lethal attacks and counterattacks to which Alex Starbuck himself had eventually fallen victim, leaving Jessie to fight on, aided by Ki, the mysterious half-Japanese, half-American warrior who had pledged his life to Alex. When Alex was killed, Ki's allegiance had gone to Jessie, whom he had known since she was a young girl, and whom he thought of almost as a sister, but as much more too, his emotions complicated by the strict *bushido* code that governed his relationship with her.

As they gazed down the twin ribbons of the rails extending in a straight, unbroken line to the eastern horizon, the train appeared in the distance, visible first only as a tiny black smoke-smudge and growing slowly, becoming discernible finally as a straight-stacked 4-4-2 locomotive pulling a full complement of baggage and passenger cars. With a rush of steam and a squealing of brake shoes on its steel wheels, the train pulled to a stop and discharged the two or three passengers disembarking at Sarah. Jessie and Ki took a final look at the platform of the station to make sure their baggage was being loaded onto the train.

"I guess that's it," Jessie said to Ki, and they stepped up into one of the passenger cars.

They'd just settled themselves in the high-backed plush seats, and were looking out the windows at the sunbaked Southwest Texas prairie that was slipping past, when the conductor came down the narrow aisle and stopped beside them, touching the bill of his cap in greeting.

"Miss Starbuck. And Ki," he said, taking the tickets they held out to him. "I saw you standing out on the platform as we pulled in. You haven't ridden with me for quite some time."

"Yes, it's been a while since we've traveled west, Mr. Brown," Jessie replied. "Most of the time we've been going in the other direction."

"And I see you're going all the way to California this trip," Brown said, as he punched the tickets and returned them.

"California's just the first leg," Ki said. "We've got more traveling ahead than I really like to think about."

"Well, we've put on something on this run that ought to make your trip a lot more pleasant," Brown said. "These new Pullman sleeping cars have drawn so much passenger traffic to the SP that we've had to add a diner."

"But this train's always had a dining car," Ki said.

"I guess I wasn't very clear, Ki," the conductor said. "I mean another diner. We've got one at the head of the train, for the day coaches, and one's been added back here for

17

the Pullman passengers. It's the next car back of this one, between it and the observation car."

"That's very thoughtful," Jessie observed. "Now we won't have to go all the way to the front of the train and wait in line at mealtimes."

"It's better than that," Brown told her. "We only have one call for meals, and really don't serve many back here, so, between times, you Pullman passengers can use it as a lounge car. With it and the observation car, you've got a chance to stretch your legs a bit."

"That will be nice," Jessie said. "Perhaps the trip won't seem quite so long if we can move around a bit."

"Make yourselves right at home, now," Brown said. "I've got a few more things to tend to, but if you need anything..."

"We'll let you know," Ki promised.

Like most veteran travelers, Jessie and Ki required very little time to get settled for the five-day train ride. Inside the large suitcase each of them had brought, they had packed small train cases. These handbag-sized cases held their personal travel needs, and once the cases had been removed, their large suitcases were stowed under the Pullman seats.

Jessie glanced out the window at the arid, featureless land through which the train was passing. Looking back at Ki, she said, "It seems a long time since I got up this morning, and they'll be serving dinner in another hour or so. I think I'll have a short nap."

"You won't mind if I leave you by yourself, then," Ki said. "You know the first thing I like to do when we get on a train for a long trip."

"Go ahead and inspect the day-coach passengers, Ki," she said. "I'll be perfectly all right."

Ki left, walking at a leisurely pace toward the front of the train. Jessie leaned back against the seat's high headrest and closed her eyes. The rhythmic clicking of the wheels as they rolled over the rail joints had an almost hypnotic effect. She was asleep within a few minutes.

Jessie woke to find Ki sitting across from her. She glanced out the window, where the purple hues of sunset colored the barren land. She said, "I didn't intend to sleep such a long time, Ki. Why didn't you wake me up?"

"There wasn't any reason to. I've only been back a few minutes. I went up to the baggage car to make sure our saddle gear was safe. But as I came through the day coaches the porter was giving the first call to dinner, so you've awakened just in time."

"I suppose that's why I woke up. I'm suddenly very hungry."

"We won't have long to wait."

As though Ki's words were a cue, a white-jacketed dining car attendant came through the rear door of the coach, tapping his high-pitched chime and giving the dinner call.

"Remember, the conductor said they only have one call back here," Jessie reminded Ki. "We'd better go to the diner."

Other passengers in the car were already starting down the aisle to the rear. Jessie and Ki were seated in the dining car before the passengers from the Pullmans ahead of theirs came in. Suddenly the diner was almost filled to capacity. Three people—two women and a man, obviously together since the women were chatting busily—came down the aisle and stopped at the table occupied by Jessie and Ki.

"You're not holding these seats for anyone, are you?" one of the women asked.

"No. Please join us," Jessie said.

Turning to the man, the woman said, "You take that vacant seat at the table across the aisle, Armand. Selma and I will sit with these people."

19

After they'd settled into their chairs, one of the women said to Jessie, "Since we're going to eat together, we might as well get acquainted. I'm Mrs. Armand Wheatley, and this is my sister, Mrs. Selma Garwich. That's my husband across the aisle."

"How do you do," Jessie said, nodding to all three of the newcomers. "I'm Jessica Starbuck, and this is Ki."

There were the usual civilized exchanges of greetings, followed by the silent consultation of menus and placing of orders. While they waited for their food to arrive, Wheatley leaned across the aisle and spoke to Jessie.

"You have an unusual name, Miss Starbuck," he said. "Are you, by any chance, related to the late financier?"

"I'm Alex Starbuck's daughter," Jessie replied. "Did you know my father?"

"I didn't know him personally," Wheatley said. "But I'm very familiar with the Starbuck name. You see, I'm—I'm in a brokerage house in Boston. My house was engaged in some joint underwriting ventures with your father's."

"Father had very little to do with the brokerage firm, and I'm afraid I'm in the same situation," Jessie said. "Ranching is more to my liking than dealing in stocks and bonds, so I spend most of my time in Texas, and that's a long way from Boston."

Alice Wheatley, seated beside Jessie, said quickly, "Please don't think my husband's being forward, Miss Starbuck. The fact is that Armand and Selma and I are addicted to whist. We've been trying, ever since we boarded this train at New Orleans, to find someone who'd be interested in making a fourth so we can play."

Before Jessie could reply, Mrs. Garwich said, "You see, Miss Starbuck, we've been told that these trains attract a large number of professional gamblers. We like the thrill of playing for money, and even though the stakes we can afford are quite small, we don't want to risk inviting just anyone to join us."

"I'm sorry," Jessie said. "I'm not really a whist addict."

"Surely you play, though?" Mrs. Wheatley asked.

"Oh, I know the game, but I don't play often. I'm afraid I wouldn't be good enough to hold my own with experts."

"We're far from experts," Wheatley protested. "But we won't press you. Of course, if you should change your mind, we'd be delighted."

"Thank you, Mr. Wheatley. If I do, I'll tell you."

Having finished their supper, Jessie and Ki returned to the Pullman car to find their berths already made up. Accustomed to early bedtime at the Circle Star, they turned in, Jessie in the lower berth, Ki in the upper.

Perhaps it was the swaying of the car, perhaps it was the constant undercurrent of noise made by the train in motion, or perhaps it was only the difference between her own bed and the Pullman berth, but Jessie was unable to sleep. Behind its heavy green curtains, the berth seemed suffocatingly hot and close. She raised the window a crack, but the stream of sooty air that swept in only made things worse. Jessie put on her clothes and slipped through the curtains. She was standing in the aisle when Ki stuck his head through the curtains.

"Is something wrong, Jessie?" he asked.

"No. I just can't seem to get to sleep. I thought I'd go back and sit on the observation platform awhile."

"Do you want company?"

"Not unless you're uncomfortable too. Don't worry about me, Ki. I think all I need is fresh air."

As Jessie entered the diner, converted now to its function as a recreation car, she saw she was not the only sleepless passenger. Since the dinner hour, the dining tables had been

21

folded down against the walls, and a half-dozen smaller tables placed at random around the car.

A beefy man occupied one table. A bulging briefcase stood open beside his chair, and the tabletop was strewn with papers. He did not even glance up at Jessie as she passed him. At another table a thin-faced, bespectacled woman was playing solitaire, engrossed in her game. A youthful couple had taken possession of one of the back corners. They had pulled their chairs together and had their heads pressed close, whispering to one another; Jessie glanced at them and at once tagged them as newlyweds.

She went on into the observation car. It was almost empty. A couple sat on one of the divans, glasses in their hands. Near the center of the car, the Wheatleys and Mrs. Garwich were playing three-handed whist. At the rear, the barkeep leaned sleepily on the small curved bar that took up one corner.

"Miss Starbuck," Mrs. Wheatley said, "I do hope you've changed your mind about joining us." She indicated the dummy hand spread on the table. "We're managing to play, but there's so much lost in three-handed bidding that it's not very enjoyable. Would you like to make our badly needed fourth?"

Somewhat to her own surprise, Jessie heard herself saying, "If you're sure you won't mind playing with a novice like me, I'd be glad to join you, Mrs. Wheatley."

"We're playing for a cent a point," Armand Wheatley said. "Small stakes, I'll grant you, but enough to add some interest to the game."

"That will suit me quite well, Mr. Wheatley," Jessie said, taking the vacant chair across from Alice Wheatley. "Shall we begin afresh, and cut for the deal?"

Like most men with a zest for life, Alex Starbuck had been a gambler. In his younger days he'd bucked the tiger

22

in the faro banks of San Francisco's wide-open gambling houses, played poker in raw Western saloons, and plunged on the high-stakes games in the gilded rooms of Canfield's famous Forty-fourth Street house in New York. He'd wagered on roulette in Macao, and fantan in the incense-laden air of sailor's haunts in other cities of the China coast.

When Alex had gotten into the bigger gamble of expanding his holdings into a worldwide financial empire, the relatively low stakes offered by the gaming table no longer lured him. He'd given up social gambling, but had seen to Jessie's education in games of chance and skill, and had taught her not only the intricacies of playing them, but the odds that faced the player.

Though she had not played whist for a good while, Jessie more than held her own from the first rubber of the game. She'd drawn Alice Wheatley as her partner, and after two or three rubbers the two of them were more than holding their own.

To her surprise, Jessie found herself growing interested in the game. The concentration it required took her mind away from the problems she'd carried from the ranch. She was astonished at how quickly the time had passed when Wheatley looked at a handsomely engraved hunter-cased watch, announced that it was close to midnight, and suggested raising the stakes to ten cents a point for a final rubber.

"Of course," Jessie agreed, glancing across the table at the tablet on which he'd been keeping the tally. "I see I'm just about even, so perhaps this will bring me out a winner."

Bidding was spirited and the play was fast. The rubber went to Jessie and her partner. Mrs. Wheatley said, "Let's not bother about settling up tonight. Why don't we just carry the score on paper, and you and I will start ahead of the game tomorrow."

23

Jessie had not thought about playing the following day, but realized that to say so would seem ungracious. "That will be fine," she said. "I've really enjoyed our game tonight."

"You're a better player than you give yourself credit for," Wheatley said. "Until tomorrow, then, Miss Starbuck."

"I'm afraid I have something unpleasant to tell you, Jessie," Ki said as they sat at dinner the following evening.

"Unpleasant? I can't think what it could be. Nothing's happened since we got on the train. Is it something you've remembered, Ki?"

"No. It's your new friends."

Jessie frowned. "The Wheatleys and Mrs. Garwich? Why, I think they're quite pleasant. I've enjoyed our whist games today, and playing seems to have relaxed me."

"That's what your card partners have planned them to do," Ki smiled. "I've been watching them while you played today. You've been playing with three slick professional gamblers, Jessie. And they're setting you up for the kill."

Chapter 3

"So tonight's the night," Ki said as he and Jessie walked back to their Pullman berths from the dining car.

"Yes. But what about the railroad detective, Ki?"

"He's on the train. He got on last night at Yuma."

"That's why you went with the conductor while I was playing cards earlier, then?"

"You weren't able to leave, so Mr. Brown took me up to the baggage car to meet him."

"What does he want me to do?"

"Just go on with your card game, the way you've been doing."

"Isn't he going to have to watch the game himself?"

"Of course he is. After you and the crooks start playing, he'll come in the observation car and sit down by me."

"And as soon as you've seen enough to prove they're cardsharps, the detective will arrest them?" Jessie asked.

"That's right. You just give me an unobtrusive signal. Oh, by the way, he wants to know if Wheatley's carrying a gun."

"I'm sure he isn't," Jessie replied. "I'd have noticed a bulge in his jacket if he was wearing a shoulder holster, and he moves too easily when he's sitting down to be wearing any kind of belt holster."

"Good. Then nobody's likely to get hurt," Ki said. "He'd like to know how much you've lost, too."

"Almost three thousand dollars. That's just for yesterday

and last night. They let me win enough to stay almost even until yesterday afternoon, then Wheatley suggested that we increase the stakes to twenty-five dollars a rubber."

Ki nodded. "The classic professional gambler's come-on. Let the sucker win until the last day or so."

Sighing, Jessie said, "It's too bad there are so many who'll take the bait, but I suppose there'll always be some who can't help themselves."

"It's just human nature, Jessie, to try to get something for nothing," Ki said. "Well, we'll give them a few minutes to get their last-minute scheming done, and then go on back."

When Jessie and Ki returned to the observation car, the Wheatleys and Selma Garwich were waiting, a fresh deck of cards in its box on the table. Slipping into the vacant chair, across from Selma, Jessie watched unobtrusively while Wheatley opened the cards. The seal on the box seemed intact, and so did the tissue that wrapped the new deck he took out.

While the cards were being spread and the draw made to determine who would deal for the beginning rubber, Jessie checked the hands of each member of the trio. All of them were still wearing the same rings she'd seen on their fingers at their first whist session. There were no new ones, which might have sharp-edged settings that could be used to put almost undetectable nicks on the edge of a playing card to mark it by suit and value.

She was certain now that the trio would not change tactics, and because she'd been watching them manipulate the cards during the four days that had passed since Ki's warning, she relaxed. Knowing that the cards would not be marked, she would not have to be alert to new methods. After four days and evenings of play, she'd become familiar with the trio's way of cheating.

26

Jessie was aware that whist offered fewer opportunities for cardsharps than most card games. Alex had showed Jessie the only two methods that were really practical. In the first, a professional sharper, relying on his trained memory, could gather the winning tricks in a preplanned sequence and stack them at a slight angle that would separate high cards from low when he halved the deck for shuffling. Then the dealer could make a false shuffle and deal from the bottom to give a confederate a hand in which the high cards had been segregated.

In the second, the cardsharp could pick up all the winning trump tricks with a single sweep of his hand and hold these segregated with a bent fingertip while performing what professional gamblers called an "intricate" shuffle. Such a shuffle kept most of the trumps together, and if he was skillful enough in dealing, the dealer could then divide the trumps between himself and his partner. This kind of deal could not be used frequently, but when used, it generally meant a clean sweep of all thirteen tricks, giving the cheater and his partner an unusually high score.

Since Ki's alert, Jessie had seen both these methods used by the Wheatley trio. However, she'd seen only Wheatley himself perform the "intricate" shuffle. This was the method used by the most skillful professional sharpers, and was among the tricks Alex had amused her with as a child. Several times during play the previous evening, she'd seen Wheatley gather the tricks with unaccustomed clumsiness or hesitation, using his fumbling to mask the swift moves in which he segregated tricks that contained high cards and placed them on the bottom of the deck.

In play, Jessie had seen those high cards come out of the hands held by Wheatley or his partner, while her hand and those of her partner contained only cards with values too low to win more than a trick or two. Invariably, when

27

Wheatley performed the "intricate" shuffle, Jessie and her partner had lost the rubber.

Until the previous day, the trio of cardsharps had been careful not to win too often; in fact, they'd favored Jessie during those first days. Now, on the final day, she waited for them to make their sweep. Midway through the first rubber, Ki came in and sat down in one of the swiveling wicker chairs across from the gaming table, and a short time later a stranger joined him. The newcomer, Jessie thought, must be the railroad detective. Both men turned their chairs away from the cardplayers, but sat at an angle that allowed them to watch the play reflected in the night-darkened observation car window.

For the first game and the two opening rubbers of the next, there was little difference between this evening's play and that of the earlier evenings. Then Wheatley made the suggestion for which Jessie had been waiting.

"Your game has improved a great deal since we first began playing, Miss Starbuck," he said. "You're certainly playing as well as any of us now."

"I suppose I just needed to get back in practice," Jessie replied. "But you and Mrs. Wheatley have been having such a good run of cards that Mrs. Garwich and I have been losing badly."

"So you have," Mrs. Wheatley agreed. "And Selma's really a better player than her scores indicate."

"We'll be arriving in San Francisco tomorrow," Wheatley said. "If you'd like to recoup your losses, we could increase the stakes a bit."

Before Jessie could speak, Selma Garwich said quickly, "I'm certainly in favor of that, Armand." Turning to Jessie, she went on, "We've had a bad run of luck, Miss Starbuck, but both of us know their good luck can't last forever."

"I suppose that's right," Jessie agreed. She turned to

28

Wheatley and asked, "How much of an increase did you have in mind, Mr. Wheatley?"

Without giving Wheatley a chance to reply, Selma asked Jessie, "Don't you think we ought to double the stakes?"

Playing her role, Jessie hesitated a moment, then said, "We're playing for twenty-five dollars a rubber now, which seemed to me like a lot when we began. I'm not sure I'd want to double that."

"Oh, come on, partner!" Selma urged. "You may not miss what we've already lost, Miss Starbuck, but I'd surely like to break even, at least. This is the last evening we'll be playing, so let's be sports and double!"

"Well..." Jessie hesitated momentarily, then said, "I suppose doubling would be all right, since it is our last evening."

"It's fifty dollars a rubber from now on, then," Wheatley said. "I think it's your deal, Miss Starbuck."

Jessie and Selma Garwich won the first rubber, but lost the next four. They won the sixth, and lost the next two. Looking across the car at Ki, Jessie caught his eye and raised her brows questioningly. Ki nodded imperceptibly, then leaned over and whispered something to the railroad detective, who watched the play on the other side of the car for a few moments, then got slowly to his feet. Stepping over to the table, he stood looking down at the players.

Wheatley picked up the trick he and his wife had just won before looking up and saying with irritation in his voice, "This is a private game, sir. Unless you have some reason—"

"All the reason I need," the detective said calmly, producing his badge. "You three are violating the state's bunco and swindling law. I'm putting you under arrest, and when we stop in Fresno, I'll turn you over to the California authorities."

"You have no right to accuse any of us of doing anything

illegal!" Wheatley protested, rising to his feet. "You have no evidence!"

"I'm afraid he has, Mr. Wheatley," Jessie said evenly. "Ki has been watching us play, and so has this detective. And I've been watching all three of you as well. Ki and I will give this man sworn affidavits that I'm sure will stand up in court."

"You'll never make such a charge stick, Miss Starbuck!" Wheatley snarled. "Even if you had a chance to—"

A whirring silver streak from across the car passed between Jessie and the detective, and Ki's *shuriken* imbedded itself in the gambler's wrist before he could drop his sleeve gun into his hand. Wheatley stood motionless, frozen in surprise, and the tiny revolver from his forearm holster dropped to the floor.

Jessie's quick eyes caught a flicker of motion from the other side of the table and leaned across it to grab Alice Wheatley's wrist before she could get her hand into her purse. With her free hand, Jessie took out the wicked little derringer the gambler's wife had tried to draw. The railroad detective whistled.

"I thought you said this fellow didn't have a gun," he said to Ki. "He had one, and now his wife turns up with another one."

Jessie replied quickly, "I gave Ki the wrong information."

"Well, Ki sure took care of your mistake, Miss Starbuck," the detective said. "Whatever kind of blade that star-pointed thing is really did the job."

Jessie went on, "I knew Wheatley didn't have a regular gun, but I didn't count on one like this." She nudged the sleeve pistol with the toe of her boot. "And I didn't count on his wife being armed, either."

"From the way they acted, being ready to shoot to avoid

being arrested, I've got a suspicion this bunch is wanted for something more serious than cardsharping," the detective said, nodding toward Wheatley, who had sunk down into a chair and was slumping there, his face ashen. His wounded arm lay stretched on the table in front of him, and he clutched it with his other hand, staring at the place where blood was oozing out around the gleaming, star-shaped disk protruding from his wrist, soaking his sleeve with a dark red stain. He was moaning softly.

The detective went on, "I reckon I'd better hustle these unholy three up to the baggage car and get the conductor to bandage this fellow's arm. We don't want him bleeding to death before he ever gets formally charged." He winked at Ki and said, "I'll see that you get your little blade back."

"Not to worry," Ki told him with a thin smile. "I've plenty more where that one came from."

Jessie looked out the window at the rugged peaks that rose on all sides of the cut through which the Northern Pacific tracks snaked their way. To the north, the flanks of the Garnet Mountains caught the golden rays of the declining sun, and to the south, the even more imposing Bitterroot Range towered in a gentle eastward arc.

Between the two ranges, the humps of lesser peaks, some no more than oversized hills, were scattered across a wide stretch of terrain, and between these lesser peaks the tracks ran like a flat, sinuous serpent. The engines at either end of the train chuffed as the rails started on a downslope and the train began to pick up speed.

"We're getting close to the mines, all right," Ki said.

He motioned toward the window, and Jessie's eyes followed his gesture. Until now the railroad tracks had wound through a thin forest of tall, wide-spread pines rising from a ground cover of stunted cedar and thick sumac. Now the

31

forest had given way to acre after acre of stumps. Wherever she looked, the raw white stubs that had once been trees rose from a landscape denuded of all vegetation. Even the low-lying, twisted cedar trees had been chopped down, and the sumac had vanished as well. Between the pine and cedar stumps was nothing but rocky, barren soil.

"Mining takes a lot of timber, Ki," Jessie said.

"Yes, I know," Ki answered, still gazing at the stubble-covered slopes. "Shoring for the tunnels, fuel for the smelters, and all that. But the last time we were here, they'd only cut down the trees within a couple of miles around the mines, and we must be ten or twelve miles from Copperopolis."

"I'll be very glad when we get there," she said. "It's been such a long time since we've been here that I'd forgotten what a trying trip it is."

After getting off the Southern Pacific in San Francisco, they'd taken a coastal steamer to Seattle, for the Southern Pacific had not yet completed its trackage beyond California to connect with the Northern Pacific's Seattle terminal. Leaving the steamer in Seattle, they'd boarded the eastbound Northern Pacific train they were now on for the final leg of their trip. Roundabout as the route seemed, because of the lack of north-south rail connections it was the quickest way to reach Montana from Southwest Texas.

"We're getting near the end of it," Ki replied. "About two more humps, and we'll be in Warm Springs. Then it's only a few more miles on the spur to Copperopolis and the mines."

"And Starhope," Jessie added. "I'm curious to see the place again, Ki. It was still very new the last time I was here, and I've been wondering how those little houses have stood up to the terrible winters."

"Your father was sure they'd do well," Ki said. "I re-

32

member that he thought Pullman's town was pretty shoddy."

"It's odd, isn't it?" Jessie said, thinking aloud. "To think that Alex started building Starhope just to win a bet with Mr. Pullman, and then got so interested in doing something for the miners working for him that he spent ten times the amount he'd have won if he'd lived."

"He'd have won the bet, though," Ki said. "And you know what that would have meant to Alex."

"Yes. But to think of him ordering more than five hundred houses built just to prove a point!"

"Well, he was determined to show Mr. Pullman that people will value something they own more than something they're just renting to use for a while."

"I know, Ki," Jessie said. "And I know that his bet with Mr. Pullman wasn't made just for sport. Alex really believed that Pullman was wrong in renting the houses in that town he built for his workers instead of selling them to the men."

"Alex believed it, of course," Ki told her. "But he was too shrewd a businessman to overlook a profit."

"You mean he expected to make money out of Starhope?"

"Of course he did, Jessie. I remember him saying once that if the mines had a twenty-percent employee turnover every four years, he'd be able to make a reasonable profit on Starhope over a twenty-year period," Ki said. "Even two-percent interest on a seven-hundred-dollar house adds up, I suppose."

"He was right, too," Jessie agreed. "While I was looking at the operating figures for the mines before we left, I looked at the Starhope figures too. Sixty percent of the mortgages have been paid off, and those that haven't were houses originally bought by men who quit their jobs at the mines later."

"They forfeited the mortgage payments and interest they'd already paid, and the company sold the houses again?"

"Of course," Jessie said matter-of-factly.

"And is Starhope showing a profit?"

"Not yet. But Alex's twenty years aren't up yet, either."

"If I could find anybody to cover my bet, I'd bet that Starhope will show a profit by then," Ki said.

"I certainly wouldn't take your bet," Jessie said. She glanced out the window, then turned to Ki and said, "We're almost there. I can see the tip of the big Anaconda smokestack just beyond the next rise."

"Then Warm Springs must be in the valley we're dropping into now," Ki said as the train picked up still more speed.

"I think it is. You know, Ki, they say mountains never really change, but these don't look the same as they did when we were here last."

"Everything changes sometime, Jessie."

"I think so too. And I've been thinking about something for the last few days, Ki. I intend to change my name when we get off this train."

"Do you think you can get away with it, Jessie?" Ki asked. "The men in the office at the mines will recognize you, even if they haven't seen you for quite a while."

"I wouldn't even *try* to fool them, but there aren't many people in Copperopolis who'd recognize me."

"No. You could get away with it there."

"To give me an excuse for asking a lot of questions, I'll say I'm a newspaper reporter from the East," Jessie said. "Marcus Daly's brought so many reporters here to write stories about the Anaconda that the people in Copperopolis shouldn't pay too much attention to another one."

"You've got it all worked out, then."

"Fairly well. I'll call myself Jessie Smith, and let everyone think I'm just another reporter that Daly's invited out."

"How are you going to explain me?" Ki asked. "Or am

34

I just going to keep out of sight and pretend we're strangers?" He thought for a moment, then added, "I don't think I'd have any trouble doing that. There are plenty of Chinese around here, and most people can't tell the difference between them and Japanese."

"Oh, I'm sure you could just sink into the background, Ki, but I need you with me."

"I suppose you've figured out how that can be done?"

"I think so. We can say you're a sketch artist, doing the pictures to go with the stories I'm supposed to write."

"Jessie, you know I can't draw a straight line!" Ki protested. "I'd never get away with it!"

"We'll find you a drawing pad of some kind. All you'll have to do is make a few scribbles on it. But you'll have to be careful not to let anybody look over your shoulder."

"I guess that would work," Ki said thoughtfully.

"I'm sure it will," Jessie said. "It'll only be for a few days, because as soon as we go out to the mine and people see us, we won't be able to get away with it any longer."

While Jessie and Ki had been talking, the train had gone across the shallow valley and was now slowing down as it mounted the next steep grade. Winding from one side to the other of the broad, steep slope, the engines chuffing and the wheels of the coaches squealing on the curves, the train reached the crest at last.

Below them spread a broad valley with a stream weaving through it. Beside the tracks at the bottom of the valley there was a small cluster of railroad shacks, and beyond them along the creek a second group of buildings were visible. Standing on a spur beside the mainline tracks there was a locomotive and a short string of cars. The spur line ran to the northwest, at a shallow angle away from the mainline. It drew their eyes to the north wall of the valley.

In the distance, towering above the valley's low wall, a

35

monstrous column thrusting high into the air dominated the skyline. It stood stark and harsh in the clear air, a plume of yellowish smoke bubbling from its tip and staining the clear sky for miles around.

"We're just about ready to stop traveling, Jessie," Ki said as they gazed at the towering stack. "That hadn't been put up the last time we were here, but I guess we've both seen enough pictures of it to know what it is."

"There's only one thing it could be," Jessie said. "The Anaconda smokestack. And even if we can't see the town from here, we know that Copperopolis isn't far from it. I'm beginning to feel better already, now that the end of our trip's so near."

Chapter 4

After leaving their luggage at the shabby baggage shed that served the spur as a depot, Jessie and Ki walked down the main and only real street of Copperopolis; the streets branching off it were more like narrow lanes, long enough to accommodate only a dozen or so houses apiece. Like the road at the switching spur where they'd boarded the accommodation train that ran between the Northern Pacific's main line and the mines, the street was unpaved.

Aside from a livery stable and a blacksmith shop at the head of the street, most of the buildings seemed to be saloons, but as Jessie and Ki got closer to the center of town they saw a general store, a doctor's office, a notions shop, a gunsmith's, and a lawyer's office. A mile or less beyond the last of the business buildings, the swirling of a thin veil of reddish-brown smoke obscured the huge bulk of the Anaconda smelter, but nothing could hide or disguise Marcus Daly's smokestack.

Dwarfing even the immense, squat red brick buildings that housed the smelter, the base of the stack could now be seen in perspective through the smoke cloud. It was almost as wide as the smelter building itself, and its gently tapering sides rose through the obscuring smoke to its crown, nearly six hundred feet above.

"I can't blame Daly for being proud of that," Jessie said thoughtfully as she and Ki made their way along the rutted street toward the center of town. "It's almost like a monument."

"Daly may think the same thing," Ki remarked.

"I'm sure he does. And don't ask me why, but now that I've seen it, I feel better about our contract with Anaconda."

"Jessie, you can't make a remark like that and not expect me to ask you to explain it," Ki said. "What does the smokestack have to do with the Starbuck mines and Anaconda?"

"Well—" Jessie frowned, trying to put her feeling into words. "Well, it's such an overpowering thing, I get an idea the man who put it up wouldn't do anything that would cause people to think badly of him. Does that make good sense, Ki?"

"It might not to some, but I think I understand what you're saying. You mentioned the contract that the Starbuck mines have with Anaconda—the one that covers the shipping of Starbuck ore to the Anaconda for smelting. I didn't know you'd been having problems with them."

"I haven't," Jessie replied. "At least none that I know of." She broke off to point ahead, where one of the buildings bore a sign proclaiming it a cafe, and a short distance farther on was the Miner's Rest Hotel. She said, "Suppose we have an early supper, Ki, then check into the hotel. I don't know about you, but I'm as hungry as a bear and feel like my clothes are lined with sandpaper. I'd like nothing better than a decent supper, and then a bath and bed."

"Whatever you say, Jessie. I could use a bite to eat."

They went into the cafe. It seemed clean, and had a half-dozen tables as well as a long counter. There were only two or three stools vacant at the counter, but two of the tables were vacant. Jessie and Ki sat down, and when the waiter came, they ordered steak and eggs—the only items on the menu besides ham and eggs and stew.

While they waited for their order to be filled, Ki said, "I suppose when you said a minute ago that you didn't know of any trouble between the Starbuck mines and the Anaconda, you were talking about the falling-off of copper production?"

Jessie nodded. "When I came here the last time, right after Alex's death, and learned that he'd agreed to contract with Anaconda to smelt all the ore from the Starbuck mines, I didn't think it was a good idea to be at the mercy of a competing company. Everything was in such turmoil then that I didn't want to change anything, so I let the agreement stand."

"Were you afraid they might use the smelting contract as a wedge to take over the mines?" Ki asked.

"Something like that," Jessie replied. "Knowing the reputations of both Hearst and Daly." She laughed, then went on, "The funny thing about the Anaconda being owned by Daly and Hearst is that the man who named it didn't even know them or anything about them."

"That's a story I've never heard," Ki said. "It was named after the snake, of course."

"Yes, but old Ben Hickey, the prospector who found the lode and started the first mine, didn't know what an anaconda was. He picked up the name from a newspaper story during the war, written when Grant captured Richmond. The story compared the Union Army to a giant anaconda swallowing the city, and Hickey thought the name was a compliment to Grant."

"Well, the name certainly fits its owners. Daly seems to be determined to swallow up everything in sight."

"I don't intend to let him or anybody else swallow the Starbuck mines, Ki," Jessie said firmly.

"Do you think that's what's in the wind, Jessie?"

"If my suspicions are correct, and the mines are in trouble, it could only come from one of two sources," she replied thoughtfully.

"Either the Anaconda or the cartel?"

"Or the two combined," she added soberly.

"Surely men like Hearst and Daly wouldn't join forces with a bunch of thieves and killers!" Ki exclaimed.

"They might if they didn't know the kind of company they were getting into. Alex didn't know what the cartel was until he'd done a lot of investigating, after they'd invited him to join them. Even then, I don't think he realized how bad it really was. If he had, he'd still be alive."

"Yes, I'm sure that's right, Jessie. If only I'd been with him that day, instead of—"

"Hush, Ki!" Jessie broke in. "We can't change the past. I know how you feel. Let's talk about—"

Whatever topic Jessie intended to suggest was put aside by the arrival of the waiter with their dinner. He set big platters in front of them. On each platter were two eggs with yolks like big yellow eyes, separated by a ridge of hash-brown potatoes from a thin fried steak the size of a stovelid.

"I'll bring you some coffee in a minute," the waiter said. "If you want biscuits, they're extra, a dime apiece."

After looking at the size of the portions, Jessie and Ki shook their heads almost in unison. After the man had gone, Jessie said, "I thought I was hungry, but I'm certainly not hungry enough to eat all this."

"That's because you didn't work up a miner's appetite by swinging a pick or shovel all day," Ki smiled. "But I didn't expect such a lot of food, either."

"We'll do our best, then," Jessie said.

For several minutes they ate hungrily, paying little attention to the coming and going of other patrons, which was a fairly constant undercurrent of activity in the small cafe. Ki stopped eating first. He pushed his plate aside and picked up his coffee cup. Sipping from it, he looked idly around the still-filled restaurant.

As he shifted his gaze around the room, he noticed that one of the men at the counter had turned to face the table where he and Jessie sat, and was staring fixedly at him. The man needed a shave; there was a two-day growth of black stubble on his heavy jaws and high cheeks. He was also *big*. His neck had the girth of an average man's thigh; his chest was immense, and he had hulking shoulders and biceps that more than filled the sleeves of his jacket. He wore the blue dungarees and loose jacket created by Levi Strauss especially for miners and prospectors.

Keeping his voice low, Ki asked Jessie, "Is there something wrong with me, Jessie? Do I look strange to you?"

Her mouth full, Jessie glanced at Ki and shook her head, then swallowed and said, "You look all right to me. Why?"

"Apparently I don't look the same to that big fellow sitting at the counter. He's staring at me as if I were a lizard or snake or something else he finds repulsive."

"Maybe it's because you're the only Oriental in the cafe," Jessie suggested. "Or maybe just because you are an Oriental."

"He ought to be used to seeing us, in this town. We both know there are a lot of Chinese working in the copper mines," Ki said. "At least there are in the Starbuck mines, and the Anaconda had about as many as we do, the last time we were here."

"Do you want to leave?"

"No. You haven't finished eating, and I don't intend to leave just because someone's staring at me."

"Then don't pay any attention to him," Jessie advised.

It was advice that Ki was not to be allowed to follow. His eyes still fixed on Ki, the hulking man raised his voice and called, "Jake!"

"What is it, Boston?" the waiter asked. "If you're in a hurry, I'm sorry, but it's going to be a minute before I can get around to you."

41

"I ain't in that big of a hurry," the man called Boston said. "Anyhow, I ain't going to eat a bite in here until you get rid of that damned chink settin' over yonder."

"Now don't be unreasonable," Jake the waiter replied. "I guess you can see he's with a lady."

"Lady, hell!" Boston grated. "She ain't no lady if she's settin' at a table with a yellow goddamn Chinaman!"

"You've got no call to say that, Boston," Jake protested. "We're in business to sell food to people. That's what they come in for, and I'd imagine they'll leave soon as they finish."

"That ain't good enough!" Boston retorted. "You go over there to that table right now and tell him to skedaddle!"

In a low voice, Jessie said to Ki, "If we don't go, that big man's going to make trouble."

"Finish your meal and take your time, Jessie," Ki told her. "We've run into things of this kind before."

"I know. But if you fight with him, it'll draw attention to us, and I'd just as soon avoid that."

"I'm sorry," Ki replied. "I'm not going to let that big bully browbeat me into leaving."

Jessie understood Ki's attitude, and knew that he could be adamant at times. She did not worry about the outcome if the big man attacked Ki. She nodded and went on eating. Ki sat calmly, unmoving, his face expressionless.

"Well, Jake, are you going to throw the chink out, or do I have to do it myself?" Boston demanded.

"Now just be patient a minute or two," Jake said. "They won't be here much longer."

"You're goddamned right they won't!" Boston snarled. He stood up and lumbered over to the table where Ki and Jessie sat. Towering above Ki, he looked down, his tiny eyes glaring.

"You heard what I said, chink," he said roughly.

"You're mistaken, sir. I am not Chinese," Ki told Boston calmly. "I am Japanese."

"That don't make no difference! You're a goddamn yellowskin, and I don't like you and your kind!"

"Nor do I like your kind," Ki said, without raising his voice. "But my dislike has nothing to do with the color of your skin, and it does not keep me from eating a meal in a public restaurant when you are present, though I admit that at these close quarters, I find the stench of your breath nauseating."

With a roar of anger, Boston reached for Ki, but his clawed hands grasped only empty air. In the instant that the big man's eyes telegraphed his intention to move, Ki had rolled out of his chair. He hit the floor, still rolling sideways, came to his feet in a single fluid motion, and stood calmly watching Boston straighten up after his futile swoop.

Throwing the chair aside, Boston lunged forward in a bull-like rush that would have sent Ki reeling if it had been completed. It was not. Ki stepped forward to meet the charge and, letting the big man's momentum add to the power of his own sinewy muscles, brought the heel of his hand up sharply under Boston's chin. The man's head snapped back, and his teeth met with a crash and a cracking of enamel as one of them shattered.

Ki's thrust staggered the hulking giant, but did not stop him. He'd been sure that a single blow would not slow Boston down much, and as his *shotei* thrust landed, he whirled aside. With a roar in which pain and anger mingled, Boston turned and started back, his arms outspread to grab Ki in a bear hug.

Taking a half-step forward, Ki braced his feet, and as Boston stretched his arms out and began to close them, still rushing forward, Ki bent from the waist, avoiding the outstretched arms that sought to close around him. He tensed

43

the sinews of his neck and lunghed forward, his head extended like a battering ram.

Boston could not slow his forward movement. Ki's head butted into the big man's solar plexus. Boston grunted as the wind rushed from his lungs, but the muscles across the big man's body had been toughened by the stresses of his job, swinging a pick and wielding a shovel. They were like bands of steel, and Boston outweighed Ki by perhaps eighty pounds.

Ki recoiled with the impact, his braced feet gave way, and he started to fall. Lightning reflexes, honed by his rigorous schooling and the discipline of constant training, enabled Ki to turn this momentary setback into another attack. As he staggered back from the shock of his collision, he dropped to the floor and snapped up his foot in a *kinteki-geri* kick. The thrusting toes of his stiffened foot stabbed into Boston's testicles.

Boston stifled a yowl of pain as his torso jackknifed forward in reaction to the kick. Still on the floor and still moving, Ki brought up his stiffened hand in a *tegatana-uchi* chop. The bottom edge of his palm smashed into Boston's nose between the tip and the bridge.

Gristle grated on bone as Ki's blow landed. Blood gushing from his broken nose, too stunned to feel the pain as yet, Boston fell on his face on the floor. Only half-conscious, he lay groaning while Ki rose to his feet in a graceful, fluid motion and stepped around the prone figure to the table, where Jessie had sat motionless during the few seconds the encounter had taken.

"He will not move for several minutes," Ki told her calmly. He was not even breathing hard from his exertions. Looking around at the others in the cafe, who were still frozen in their places, he went on, "Perhaps it would be wise for us to leave before my unworthy adversary recovers."

"I think it would be very wise indeed," Jessie said. She stood up and, with Ki at her side, stepped to the counter. Jake the waiter had not moved from the spot where he'd been standing when Boston began picking the quarrel with Ki. Jessie took several cartwheels from her skirt pocket and held them in her extended palm. She asked, "How much was our dinner?"

"Lady, if you'll just take that Chinese fellow and get outta here before Boston comes around, I won't charge you a penny," Jake replied. "But in case you don't know, Copperopolis has got a law against Chinese coming into town. If that Boston runs into your friend in here again, he's apt to wreck this place."

"Thank you, but I prefer to pay," Jessie said. "And as you heard Ki telling the man you call Boston, he is not Chinese, but Japanese."

"Chink or Jap, it don't matter to me, and it don't change the law," Jake replied. "I want the two of you to leave."

Jessie stacked four of the silver dollars on the counter, and said, "I think this should cover our bill."

"That's plenty, lady, plenty," Jake said quickly, as Boston groaned and dragged his hands along the floor. "Now just get outta here, please, will you?"

Jessie and Ki left unhurriedly. Boston was just beginning to lift himself to his hands and knees as they left. He was groaning, blood dripping from his shattered nose. Jessie and Ki stepped out into the street. Dusk was beginning to shade the eastern sky above the jagged peaks of the Rockies, and to the west, the sun's rim was touching the tips of the Bitterroots. Lying in the valley as it did, Copperopolis was already in the shade, and lamps had been lighted in some of the commercial buildings.

"I hope we won't have any trouble getting rooms at that place down the street, Ki said, nodding toward the sign above the Miner's Rest Hotel.

"Don't worry," Jessie told him. "If we do, we'll change our plans and go out to the mines. There's a little flat at the office that's set aside for visitors, and I'm sure there are rooms in the bunkhouses. But let's try the hotel here, first."

"Our bags and other gear are in the other direction, at the station," Ki reminded her. "Wouldn't it be a good idea to get them before we go to the hotel?"

"Of course. I'd forgotten. Let's go after them."

As they started to turn toward the railroad station, a man came out of the cafe behind them. "Just a minute, please!" he called. "I'd like to talk with you, if you don't mind."

Jessie and Ki turned to look back. The man who'd called to them was young, in his late twenties or early thirties. He was tall, well built, his face clean-shaven. He had a firm, square jaw, an aquiline nose, brown eyes, and light brown hair. He carried a pearl-gray derby hat in one hand, and had on a business suit rather than the rough blue denim Levi's worn by almost all the men they'd seen on the street or in the restaurant.

"What do you want to talk about?" Jessie asked.

"Well—I may be making a mistake," he said. "But my name is Fred Edmonds. I'm assistant superintendent at the Starbuck mines. And unless I'm wrong, you're Miss Jessica Starbuck."

For a moment Jessie stood silent, startled by the unexpected recognition, seeing her plans for a quietly anonymous few days of investigating Starhope and the mines going up in smoke. She had recalled Edmonds name as having been signed to some of the reports she received from the mines, and realized instantly that it would be foolish to deny her identity to anyone employed there who'd seen her and recognized her.

She nodded and said, "Yes, I am. And since you've

recognized me, I'm sure you must remember Ki."

"I do, of course," Edmonds replied. "But I'm afraid you've forgotten me, Miss Starbuck. That's understandable, of course. The last time you were here, I was working in the office as a clerk. I've been promoted since then, as I'm sure you know."

"Yes. You've signed some of the operating reports I've seen, and now that I know what you were doing earlier, I recall having seen you. Did you want something special, Mr. Edmonds?"

"Well—" Edmonds hesitated. "I really acted on impulse, Miss Starbuck. It just seemed unfriendly, somehow, not to speak to you and see if there's any way I can be helpful."

"We've only been here a short time, Mr. Edmonds," Jessie said. "Ki and I were starting for the station to pick up our luggage, and then we were planning to see if we can get rooms at the hotel down the street."

"You mean the Miner's Rest, of course," Edmonds said. "You certainly won't have any problem. We rent two rooms there on a permanent basis, for business visitors and for times like this evening, when I'd planned to stay here instead of going back to the mines. I'll just get a room for myself, and you and Mr. Ki can use those we rent permanently. But had you forgotten that there's a flat at the mines, just for company officials who're here on a visit?"

"No. I hadn't overlooked that," Jessie replied. She'd been taking stock of Edmonds and decided that the only solution to her problem was to take him into her confidence. She went on, "I didn't plan to go to the mines at once, Mr. Edmonds. Suppose you walk down to the station with Ki and me. We'll get our luggage and go back to the hotel, and then we'll talk. I have a hunch that I'm going to take you up on your offer to help us."

Chapter 5

As the three started down the street, Ki said, "Jessie, you and Mr. Edmonds will want to talk. I'll go ahead and get the luggage assembled, so that we won't waste any time."

"Thank you, Ki," Jessie replied. When Ki stepped up his pace and drew ahead of them, she turned to Edmonds and said, "I planned to stay here in Copperopolis for a few days before going to the mines, and I didn't want anyone to know I was here, Mr. Edmonds. In fact, I planned to use another name until I was ready to go to the office."

"I hope I haven't upset your plans by pushing myself—" Edmonds began.

Jessie silenced him with a quick gesture. "Not at all. But I'm going to ask you not to mention to anyone that I'm here. That includes Mr. Mason."

His voice showing that he was puzzled by Jessie's request, Edmonds replied, "I'll do whatever you ask, of course, Miss Starbuck. But Mr. Mason—"

"Loyalty to your superior does you credit, Mr. Edmonds," Jessie broke in. "I hope you can reconcile that with the fact that your greatest loyalty is to the Starbuck mines."

"I'm not forgetting," Edmonds replied, a bit stiffly. "And that means you, of course, as their owner." When Jessie made no reply, he went on, "As it happens, there's no problem. Mr. Mason left by the afternoon train. He'll be in the capital for a few days. The legislature is thinking of revising mine safety rules, and he wanted to talk to some of the members. But even if he was here, I'd certainly honor your request."

"Thank you. If you're wondering why I don't want to advertise that I'm here, one of my reasons for making the trip is to talk to some of the people living at Starhope."

"You're not thinking of changing things there, are you?"

"No, indeed. My father started the idea of providing our workers with good houses that they could buy on reasonable terms, and I'm as interested in maintaining it as he was."

"Starhope's been a really wonderful thing for my own family, Miss Starbuck," Edmonds said earnestly. "I'd hate to see anything happen to it."

"I'm interested in why you should say that. Would you mind telling me?"

"Of course not. My father was killed in a train wreck while I was away at school. My mother would have had no place to go if Father hadn't bought a house in Starhope, and I'd have been forced to leave school to provide for her. By working hard and squeezing every penny, I managed to finish school, and got a job in the office at the mine. And, well, I've worked my way up to my present job as a result."

Jessie nodded. "I'm glad you told me that, Mr. Edmonds. It was for just that sort of situation that my father built Starhope."

They'd reached the station by now. Ki had brought the suitcases out to the narrow platform; he picked up both of them, but Edmonds insisted on taking Jessie's. They started back toward town, Jessie walking between the two men.

After they'd gone a short distance, Edmonds said to Ki, "I was very impressed by the way you handled Boston in the cafe, Mr. Ki. You made it look so easy."

"It looks that way, but learning the art isn't easy," Ki replied. "And please, I'm not used to being called 'mister.' Just call me Ki—I'd like that better."

49

"Of course," Edmonds replied. He went on, "Boston will be looking for revenge, though. You'd better keep your eyes open."

"Thank you, I will."

"Does this man you call Boston work at the Starbuck mines?" Jessie asked. "He seems to me to be a born troublemaker, as bullies so often are."

"He worked for us for a while, Miss Starbuck," Edmonds said. "And you're right in judging him to be a troublemaker. We had to fire him. He found a job at the Anaconda and may still be working there, but I don't really think he is. I've seen him with Saul Goodwin a great deal lately, and I have a hunch that the Anaconda had to fire him too, and that Goodwin's hired him."

"Who is Saul Goodwin?" Jessie asked.

"Haven't you heard of him?" Edmonds sounded surprised. "I'd have thought Mr. Mason would have included some mention of him and the Knights of Labor in his reports."

It was Jessie's turn to be surprised. "You mean Goodwin is trying to get our men to join the Knights of Labor?"

"Why, yes. He's been here for several months, talking about the union to our miners and the ones at the Anaconda mines and the smelter."

"This is the first I've heard of it," Jessie said.

"I'm sure Mr. Mason had a good reason for not bringing it to your attention, Miss Starbuck," Edmonds said. "If you ask him about Goodwin, though, it'll put me in a—"

"A difficult position?" Jessie finished for him. Then she smiled. "Don't worry. I won't tell Mr. Mason that you mentioned Goodwin to me."

"It's not that he'd mind, I'm sure," Edmonds said, sounding uncomfortable. "I simply spoke without thinking and without knowing that you hadn't had a report on it."

"I understand your situation, Mr. Edmonds, and I certainly don't blame you for not wanting me to mention to Mr. Mason where I heard about this Goodwin and the union."

"Speak of the devil," Edmonds said. "There's Goodwin now, just coming out of that saloon." He pointed to a short, stocky man who, as he emerged from a saloon a short distance ahead, stood silhouetted against the light that flooded from the open door.

"Let's step into the shadow of that building," Jessie said quickly.

They were only a few steps from the black shadow thrown by the closed building, a doctor's office, and they reached the dark area before Goodwin noticed them. Jessie studied the union organizer as he stopped outside the saloon to light a cigar.

As the match he struck flared up, Jessie got a clear look at his face. He had high cheekbones, and his face had probably been craggy at one time, but was now becoming chubby. He wore a neatly-trimmed beard and had a broad, jutting nose, but the match was extinguished before Jessie could see his most revealing feature, his eyes, for when the flame died away they were hidden in the shadow cast by the brim of his high-crowned derby hat.

He turned his head, looking up and down the street, the smoke from his cigar trailing through the air. The cloud of smoke caught the light from behind and veiled Goodwin's face, so Jessie had no chance to get a second clear look at him.

"Well," Edmonds said after a moment. He gestured at the bulky form of Boston coming toward them. "Perhaps it's just as well that we stopped here in the shadow."

They watched while Boston approached. As he drew closer, they could see that he was wearing a bandage that covered most of his face, a wide swath of white that started

51

just below his eyes and extended to his upper lip. Boston stopped when he came up to Goodwin, and the two men talked for a few moments, Goodwin gesticulating angrily, but Jessie and her group were too far away to hear what they were saying. Then, walking side by side, they moved off down the street, turned into one of the side lanes, and vanished.

"That's Third Avenue they've turned down," Edmonds said. "Goodwin's rented a house there, and unless I'm badly mistaken, that's where they're going."

"I'd say your guess about Boston working for Goodwin was a pretty shrewd one," Jessie told Edmonds as they resumed walking toward the Miner's Rest.

"It's still just a guess, though," Edmonds said. "I don't know for a fact that Goodwin's paying him anything. They might just be friends."

"A man like Boston has no friends," Ki said quietly. "If Goodwin has anything to do with him, it's because Boston is doing some kind of work for him."

"I think we need to find out more about Saul Goodwin, Ki," Jessie said thoughtfully. Then she turned to Edmonds and asked, "Do you know more about him than you've already told us?"

"A little." They'd reached the Miner's Rest by now. It was a rambling two-story structure, and Jessie took it as a good omen that it had been painted recently. Edmonds hesitated for a moment before going in. "I think it would be better if we talked about him inside, though, instead of standing here in the street. I don't know the full extent of your plans, Miss Starbuck, but if you want to keep your identity secret, we shouldn't be seen together here in Copperopolis."

"Yes, that's a good point," Jessie agreed. "Let's get settled first, then we'll meet in one of our rooms and talk."

"You and Ki won't have to sign the register," Edmonds went on. "I'll tell the manager that you're guests of the Starbuck management, and get another room for myself for tonight."

"I suppose it's too much to hope for a room with a private bath and running water," Jessie said.

"I'm afraid it is. But if you're thinking of a hot bath after your trip, I can tell the manager to have the tub filled for you later on."

"I'd appreciate that. Say a half hour from now?" Then Jessie thought of something else. She said, "I hope the hotel has its own dining room. Surely the restaurant where we ate tonight isn't the best that Copperopolis has to offer."

"They serve breakfast and supper here," Edmonds replied. "And the dining room isn't open to the public, but only to guests of the hotel. You won't have to worry about anything except finding a place to have your noon meal."

"That won't be any problem at all," Jessie replied. "Ki and I will be out at noon, so we'll just buy something at the grocery store to make up a cold lunch."

"We'll go in and you can get settled, then," Edmonds said.

"Give me ten minutes to freshen up," Jessie said. "Then we'll meet in my room and talk."

Ki tapped at Jessie's door first. He said, "We seem to have gotten here just in time, Jessie."

"Yes. It's my fault, of course, that things are happening here which I don't like. I should have come and taken a look at the mines long before now." Then she asked, "What do you think of Fred Edmonds, Ki?"

"He has a great deal to learn, but I think he also has the ability to learn it. All in all, he's a very capable man."

Jessie nodded. "Yes. And perhaps we got here at a very

lucky time, Ki. It gives me a chance to look into the operation of the mines and to check on Starhope without Jared Mason being here to guide me along whatever path he'd prefer me to follow."

"You don't trust Mason?" Ki asked.

"I don't know what to think about him yet, Ki. Those last operating reports really worry me. So does his failure to say anything about this man Goodwin being here."

A light rapping on the door interrupted her. Jessie nodded to Ki, who opened the door to admit Fred Edmonds.

"Sit down, Mr. Edmonds," Jessie said. "I'm curious to hear what you have to tell me about Goodwin and the Knights of Labor."

"I'm afraid there's very little for me to tell," Edmonds replied. "We know Goodwin's the boss here, but we don't know a great deal about what he's really doing."

"Have you talked to the managers at the Anaconda?" Jessie asked. "They hire a lot more men than we do, with the smelter as well as their mines."

"Mr. Mason's talked to them," Edmonds replied. "They don't know any more than we do, Miss Starbuck. Perhaps less. They've got so many men that it's harder for them to keep an eye on their workers than it is for us. We run ten men in our underground gangs, and there are fifteen in the Anaconda's gangs."

"What about the smelter?" Jessie asked.

"There are even bigger gangs and fewer foremen in the smelter than in the mines," Edmonds said. "Their smelter gangs have twenty or twenty-five men in them."

"But you do know that Goodwin's trying to organize them too?" she frowned.

"Oh, yes indeed. But he's concentrating on us, Miss Starbuck. Our men stay longer, while the Anaconda crews change a lot. But Goodwin works behind closed doors and in the dark."

"You must hear gossip, talk of some sort," Jessie insisted.

"We hear a lot of rumors, but that's all. Even the foremen and supervisors in the mines haven't been able to learn much."

"Surely, with as many men as there are working in the mines, there are some who'll talk," Ki said with a frown.

"I don't think you and Miss Starbuck understand how Goodwin works," Edmonds said. "Goodwin doesn't come into the mines himself. The work of recruiting members is done by miners he's persuaded to join. And they just talk to the man working next to them, cutting face in a tunnel, or filling an ore cart."

"Then you can't be sure there's any talking being done at all, can you?" Jessie asked.

"Only by the gossip we pick up," Edmonds agreed. "And they don't talk. They've heard about the Molly Maguires back in the East, and what they did to miners the union blacklisted."

"Yes, I've heard about the Molly Maguires too," Jessie said. "The miners called them enforcers. They were a bad lot."

"I'm afraid I don't understand what the Molly Maguires were, or what they did," Ki said. "I've never heard of them before."

"They operated several years ago," Jessie said, "when a few miners back East, in the Pennsylvania coal mines, tried to organize a union. Most of the miners didn't want one, and those who did tried to make them join. I remember how indignant Alex was when he heard about it. He said no man should be forced to join anything he didn't want to."

"Where do the Molly Maguires come in?" Ki asked.

"They were a bunch of plug-uglies the union hired to terrorize and kill the ones who were against them," Jessie explained.

"I don't suppose the union was very popular, then."

"No. It died very quickly. But a lot of the men who were behind it are running the Knights of Labor now."

Turning to Edmonds, Ki asked, "There hasn't been anything like that happening here, has there?"

"Not yet. But now that Boston seems to be working for Goodwin, I'm afraid things may change for the worse."

"I don't like the idea of our men being threatened," Jessie said. "Or being forced to do something they don't want to, because they're afraid of what might happen to their families. I wouldn't object to them organizing a union, but I wouldn't want the union controlled by anyone such as this Goodwin seems to be. If he's hired that man Boston, I'm afraid we might see something like the Mollie Maguires here."

Ki said thoughtfully, "Since nobody in authority at the mines seems to know what's happening, Mr. Edmonds, I'd think you might be interested in finding out."

"I'm sure Mr. Mason would," Edmonds replied.

After a moment, Ki said, "You don't turn away a man looking for a job just because he happens to be Japanese or Mexican or black, do you?"

Before Edmonds could answer, Jessie said quickly, "No, Ki! I will not have you going into the mines as a spy!"

"Why not, Jessie?" he asked. "It's a sure way of learning what's really going on. Maybe it's the only way."

"I don't intend to do anything before I talk to Jared Mason, and see what he's learned about Goodwin," Jessie said firmly.

"I think I can tell you as much as Mr. Mason knows, Miss Starbuck," Edmonds volunteered. "We don't know anything except that he showed up here several months ago, and very soon after he arrived, we began hearing rumors in the office that he was trying to organize a chapter of the

Knights of Labor. The people at the Anaconda heard the same rumors, but neither one of us has been able to find out a great deal."

"If you're really interested in finding out—" Ki began.

Jessie interrupted again. "No, Ki. We have other things to do. We know now what Goodwin's up to, so let's forget him for a while and go on with our original plan." She turned to Edmonds. "Remember, now, you're to say nothing to anyone in the office at the mine about Ki and me being here."

"Yes, I understand that, Miss Starbuck."

"I'm going to call myself Jessie Smith for the next few days, and pose as a reporter for a New York newspaper. Ki will be an artist who's doing sketches to go with my stories. I'll spend most of my time in Starhope, so don't look for me to visit the mine until I've finished talking to the women there. And until I do come to the mine, Mr. Edmonds, you will please forget that you saw me here in Copperopolis."

"I understand that too," Edmonds said. "You can depend on me to do what you've told me to."

"I'm sure I can. Now I know you have a busy day ahead, so I think we'd better say good night."

After Edmonds had gone back to his room, Jessie told Ki, "We may have walked into more than we bargained for when we planned this trip."

"We couldn't have come here at a better time, though," he pointed out.

"No," she agreed. "But it seems the more we uncover, the more we find that needs to be uncovered."

"Speaking of uncovering things, I still think my idea of going into the mines as a laborer could get us a lot of information that we need about Goodwin."

"No, Ki. I want you to stay with me, and both of us to

stay away from Goodwin. Whatever he has up his sleeve can wait. It's not as important as finding out what's going on in our own backyard, why copper production's down, what that letter I got about Starhope means."

"There's no way you can trace an anonymous letter, Jessie. Whoever wrote it didn't intend for you to find out who they are."

"That isn't going to stop me from trying," she said. "But that's tomorrow's job."

"Of course," Ki replied. "We'll talk about it at breakfast, then. Good night, Jessie."

Jessie had not realized how tired she was until she came back to her room from the bathroom at the end of the hall, where she'd soaked until the water in the tub began to cool. She took her Colt out of her suitcase and slipped it under the pillow, then walked across the room to the dresser to blow out the coal-oil lamp. Returning in the darkness to the bed, she let her robe slip to the floor and dropped on the bed. The mattress could have been softer and less lumpy, but Jessie was beyond caring. Pulling the sheet up, she snuggled her head into the pillow and was asleep in a few seconds.

Chapter 6

"I'm glad it's only four miles to Starhope," Jessie said as she and Ki lurched and bounced over the ruts in the road leading to the Starbuck mines. They were riding in a buggy Jessie had rented from the Copperopolis livery stable. "The old carts they hauled ore in to the smelter before the railroad spur was built didn't leave much of this road."

"Maybe we should've started earlier," Ki remarked as he pulled sharply on the reins to turn the horse away from a set of ruts that threatened to upset the buggy.

"I couldn't seem to get wide awake," Jessie said. "Yesterday was unusually long and busy."

"Yes, I'll admit our days on the Circle Star are vacations, compared to traveling and running into people like the Wheatleys and Boston," Ki nodded.

"Every time we go on one of these trips, I can understand better why Alex loved the ranch as he did. But these mines and the other things he created were as much a part of him as the Circle Star. And they all go together, I suppose."

"Do you have any plan to follow when we get to Starhope?" Ki asked. "Or will you jusk knock on doors here and there and ask your questions?"

"What I'm hoping for is to mix in a few questions that might lead us to whoever wrote that letter."

"You're looking for a needle in a haystack, then."

"I suppose so," Jessie admitted. "Still, it's a small haystack compared to some we've found things in."

59

"You do have one good clue," Ki remarked thoughtfully after they'd ridden for a few minutes in silence.

"What's that?"

"Why, whoever wrote the letter must be somebody who's lived in Starhope since Alex built it. You said the other night that about sixty percent of the mortgages have been paid off. There are five hundred houses in Starhope, but you only need to be concerned with a little more than half of them."

"When you put it that way, it doesn't sound like such a big job," Jessie said, smiling. Then, more soberly, she added, "But that's still three hundred houses, Ki."

"We'll just have to hope for a lot of luck, then."

It was late in the morning when they saw Starhope from a distance through the thin bushes that stood in patches on the rough terrain. While the pines in that area of the Rockies had never grown thickly, the vegetation here was even thinner than elsewhere, because most of it was second-growth saplings and brushy ground cover.

Long ago, the bigger trees had been cut; they had provided shoring timbers for the Starbuck copper mines, as well as fuel to power the hoists and to build and heat the worker's camps that had dotted the slopes before Starhope was built.

After the coming of the railroad, the wood needed for mine timbers and building lumber had become less costly, and coal could be shipped in cheaply for fuel. Then the cutting of trees in the area of the mines had stopped, but the thin second-growth trees were widely spaced and spindly. Years still lay ahead before the forest would be restored to its original state.

"There it is!" Jessie said, pointing to the rows of neatly painted gray houses that had suddenly come into view as

60

the buggy topped a rise in the road. She and Ki looked down into a little saucerlike valley. "Pull up, Ki, and we'll decide how we're going to work our way through the town when we get there."

Ki reined in, and they sat looking down at Starhope. The town covered a roughly rectangular area almost a mile long and three-quarters of a mile wide. Its houses were spaced in neat rows on a gently sloping shelf that looked down into the small oval valley. On the hillside above the town stood a small water tank. Starhope's houses were not all exactly alike, though a close observer would have noted after a few minutes that the pattern of their construction was repeated often.

Light gray was the predominant color of the exterior walls, with a few that had been repainted in brighter hues: green, tan, and two or three that were a dazzlingly conspicuous railroad yellow. The dark, weathered shingles of the roofs pulled the little group of houses together into a sort of unity.

Surveying the area around Starhope after she'd absorbed the view of the town itself, Jessie saw the tracks of the railroad spur. The twin lines of wheel-polished steel ran around the perimeter of the valley, then headed straight over the next hump to the Starbuck mines, a half-mile distant.

All that was visible of the mines from where Jessie and Ki sat was a corner of the main office building. Her memory refreshed by a view that she had not seen for several years, Jessie remembered now that the three mineshafts opened on the slope of the valley that began just past the office.

"It's close to noon," she said, glancing at the sun that hung above the scanty trees. "Since we've stopped here, it's as good a place as any to have a bite of lunch before we start work."

Ki reached under the buggy seat and brought out a paper

61

sack and a small jug. He opened the sack and took out a packet wrapped in butcher's paper, broke the string, and opened it to reveal a slab of cheese and a six-inch length of summer sausage. Placing the bag on the seat between him and Jessie, Ki slid his *tanto* from its sheath in the waistband of his trousers.

"Help yourself to crackers. The clerk put them in the bag loose," he told Jessie.

Spreading the thick paper in which the sausage and cheese had been wrapped, he cut thin slices from the sausage. Then he wiped the knife carefully and slid it back into the sheath. He broke the slab of cheese into small pieces and waved his hand over the meager spread.

"This isn't exactly a feast," Jessie said. "But we've done a lot worse at times."

"So we have. And if the breakfast we had at the hotel was any indication, we'll have a better supper this evening than we did yesterday."

They ate in companionable silence that was broken only by the occasional grunting wheeze of a spruce grouse or the high-pitched *took-zeeee* of a mountain thrasher. Jessie ate lightly and finished first. She pulled the cork from the jug and drank two or three swallows of water, then moistened a corner of her bandanna and wiped the grease from her fingers.

"Enough is as good as a feast, some philosopher once said, so I suppose we can say we've feasted."

Ki did not reply; his mouth was full. He finished chewing and swallowed, then said, "After the breakfast we had, I'm not terribly hungry myself. But since I got only a few bites of dinner last night, I overdid it at breakfast, too."

They covered the rest of the distance to Starhope in a very short time. Ki pulled up at the first row of houses and said, "I suppose this is as good a place as any to start."

"It suits me fine," Jessie replied. "Get your sketchpad, and we'll see what we can find out."

Selecting a house at random, Jessie tapped at the door. A middle-aged woman in a house dress and apron opened it and cocked her head in frank curiosity while she studied Jessie and Ki for a moment before speaking.

"What do you want?" she asked. "If you're peddling patent medicine or pills, you might as well go on along, because we got a lot more of 'em than we'll ever swallow."

"We're not selling anything," Jessie said quickly. "My name is Jessie Smith. I'm a reporter from the *New York Herald,* and Ki is an artist who's drawing pictures to go with my stories."

"Stories about what?" the woman asked.

"About Montana, and what it's like to live here. Especially in a town so far away from everything."

"Laws, we're not far away from things anymore, not since the railroad's come in. Why, we can get on the cars and be just about anyplace in a week or two."

"Then you don't mind if I ask you a few questions about what it's like to live here, in a company town?"

"Well, I don't guess it'd hurt anything. Only don't go calling Starhope a company town. Us folks that lives in these houses *owns* 'em, lock, stock, and barrel. It ain't like them company towns the Anaconda's got, because the Starbuck bosses can't tell us what to do. But if you want to talk, you might as well come in, where you can set down and be comfortable."

"Thank you. That would be very nice."

They followed the woman into a room that was neat but sparsely furnished. It held a divan, three chairs, and a small round table. In one corner stood a woodburning stove, its pipe rising and curving into a flue in the wall. The woman motioned to the sofa. Jessie sat down, but Ki did not. He

63

stood holding his sketchpad and pencil.

"Ain't you going to set, Mr. Ki?" the woman asked.

"If you don't mind, I'd like to be able to move around, so that I can find the best angles for drawing," Ki said, though of course his true reason was to keep her from seeing that he was producing only scribbles.

"Whatever you say. Well, start asking, Miss Smith," she said, settling into one of the chairs. "I still don't understand why you want to talk to me, but I'll do my best to tell you whatever you want to know."

"I'd like to know your name, to start with," Jessie said, taking out her notebook.

"Oh. I guess you forget about introducing yourself when you live in a place like this one here, where everybody knows everybody else. I'm Samantha Carruthers. Missus John Carruthers, I guess is how city folks put it."

"Your husband works at the Starbuck mines, I suppose?"

"Sure does. In Number Three. He's a tunnel bracer. You know what that is, I guess?"

"I think so. I know that the mine ceilings have to be braced with timber posts," Jessie said. "Have you lived in Starhope long?"

"Since Mr. Alex Starbuck built it. Got our house all paid out, and we own it now," Mrs. Carruthers said proudly.

"Did you have any trouble making the payments?"

"Well, keeping 'em up squeezed us a time or two. And once we got behind, when John was hurt and couldn't work for a month. But the office said it was all right for us to be late paying."

"What about your neighbors?" Jessie asked.

"Why, they're folks just like us. We get along."

"Have you heard of any trouble that might be threatening the town here, Mrs. Carruthers?"

"Only gossip, folks flapping their jaws. But there's always gossip. I don't pay it no mind."

"What kind of gossip?"

"Oh, like always. Saying things are going to change, or that they're going to stay the same. Some says one thing, some says another. Right now they're saying if the union catches hold here, Mr. Starbuck's daughter—she's the one that owns the mines now, you know—she might sell out to Anaconda, and they'd close Starhope down."

"How could they do that, if you own your house?" Jessie asked, frowning. "How can they put you out of a house you own?"

"You know, Miss Smith, that's what I keep asking myself. Besides, there's some that says just the opposite."

"What's that?" Jessie asked.

"Them as favors the union says that if the men don't join it, Miss Starbuck can cut their pay whenever she takes a notion to, and then the ones that ain't got their houses paid up won't be able to make their payments."

"What do you think, Mrs. Carruthers?"

"Me? Like I told you, I hear the talk, but I don't pay heed to it."

"Do many of your neighbors pay attention to it?" Jessie asked.

"A few does. And there's some been scared by all the things the union men have been saying."

"But it hasn't caused any disturbances in Starhope? Fights, arguments, things of that kind?"

"Laws, no! Oh, there's been some hot words spoke, mostly by the men. But nothing you'd call real serious."

"Then you're not worrying about what might happen?"

"Not a mite. It's like my husband says. Long as there's ore to be dug out, there's going to be men needed to dig it, and it don't matter whether they're working for Miss Starbuck or the Anaconda, they'll have jobs."

"Then you think most of the men don't feel that they need a union?" Jessie asked.

For the first time, Mrs. Carruthers seemed uneasy. She sat silent for a moment, then asked Jessie, "This newspaper you work for—it don't belong to the union, does it?"

"No."

"Then I'll speak plain. Most men just don't care. Now it might not be that way at the Anaconda, where the foremen are a mite stricter, but that's the way it is here."

Closing her notebook, Jessie stood up and said, "I think that's all I need to ask you, Mrs. Carruthers. Thank you for talking with me."

"No thanks needed or expected, Miss Smith. Always glad to have somebody new to talk to."

Outside, Jessie stood for a moment, looking along the neat row of houses, before she asked Ki, "Did you notice that she kept talking about things changing here at Starhope, but didn't seem too worried about it?"

"Yes. But I'm not sure I know what that means, Jessie."

"Neither do I. But maybe we'll get an idea after we've talked to a few more people."

For the balance of the afternoon, as Jessie and Ki moved at random from one house to another, they heard much the same things that Mrs. Carruthers had told them. At last, with the sun dipping behind the valley's rim, Jessie decided to give up.

"Let's go back to town, Ki," she sighed as they got into the buggy after an especially long interview. "I feel like I've been groping through a fog. Everyone we've talked to feels that something's going on, but even if they don't know what it is, they don't seem very worried."

"There's something brewing, all right," Ki said thoughtfully as he turned the buggy onto the road to Copperopolis. "And it certainly concerns the mines. Your hunch was right,

Jessie. We didn't make a mistake in coming here."

Jessie shook her head. "But I still don't have anything solid. Just a feeling. And I don't think I have a chance of finding whoever it was that wrote that letter. Not among so many people."

"What do you intend to do, then?"

"Drop my plan and be myself. Jessie Smith can't do much more than we've done today. Jessie Starbuck can go into the mine office and ask questions and look at records. Maybe I can dig up what I'm looking for that way."

"Are you sure now what you're looking for?"

"No. But I'm sure there's something at the bottom of this feeling that we've uncovered today."

"It might be that Goodwin's agitation has been stirring up the people," Ki suggested.

"I'm sure that has something to do with it. But I don't think that's all. Something's wrong at the mines. And I mean to find out what it is."

As Jessie and Ki sat at supper in the small, quiet dining room of the Miner's Rest, Ki said, "I've been thinking, Jessie. I'm sure there are some of my countrymen, and some Chinese as well, working at the Starbuck and Anaconda mines. Perhaps if I talked to them, I might find out something helpful."

"Do you think they'd know any more than the women I've visited today?"

"They might. Men gossip just like women do, you know, but they do their talking on the job. And they don't always watch what they say in front of Orientals. They seem to have the idea that Japanese and Chinese don't understand English."

"It's worth trying," Jessie said. "But how would you find out where they are?"

Ki smiled. "That won't be hard. Even though they might hate each other in their own countries, in the States they're all treated the same way, and they tend to settle close together for their own protection. Somewhere close to town there's sure to be an Oriental neighborhood. They'd clam up if you or any other American tried to talk to them, but I think I can get them to talk to me. I speak Japanese, remember, and even a little Cantonese and Mandarin, though I'm a bit rusty."

"I'm ready to grasp at any straw, Ki. It's worth a try."

"Unless you have plans for us to ask more questions somewhere this evening, I'll snoop around."

"I don't have a thing in mind, Ki. I'm going to bed early."

"Then I'll see what I can find out."

Ki left the Miner's Rest shortly after he and Jessie had finished dinner. The evening was young; darkness had just settled down. It was still the supper hour in Copperopolis, and the street was deserted, though lights were spilling out from the cafe and saloons and the general store. After his brush with Boston, Ki was sure he'd find no welcome in any of the saloons, even if his only reason for going in was to ask where the town's Orientals lived. He walked down to the general store and went inside.

A lone clerk was at the counter, making change for the only customer, a woman, whose purchases were stacked on the counter. Ki couldn't help noticing her. She wore an elaborate dress of electric-blue satin with creamy lace decoration; a small toque was perched at a jaunty angle on her upswept blond hair, and even at a distance Ki could see the rouge on her cheeks and lips. He mentally tagged her as being from one of the bordellos that occupied their own little enclave at the edge of town.

He stopped just inside the door and stepped behind the edge of a rack displaying knives and other cutlery, while he waited for the clerk to wrap the woman's packages. The clerk was in no hurry; he dawdled at the job of assembling the goods on the counter into a compact pile for wrapping, while his eyes darted from the counter to the customer.

At last the wrapping was completed. The clerk handed the package across the counter, and the woman turned to go just as heavy footsteps thudded through the door. Ki peered around the edge of the cutlery rack. Boston was just entering the store.

Ki moved back quickly. He was certain that Boston would attack him on sight, and he did not want another purposeless confrontation with the big man. Boston stopped just beyond the cutlery rack, directly in the path of the woman, who was heading for the door.

"Well, hello, beautiful!" Boston said in his hoarse, grating voice. "You must be new in town, because I sure ain't seen you before. Which one of the places you working in? I'd like to come see you later on."

"I beg your pardon?" the woman said icily. She turned to look behind her and added, "Surely you aren't speaking to me."

"Ah, come off it, girlie!" Boston said. "I been around enough to know what line of business you're in. Now just tell me where you work, and I'll drop by after while."

"Please stand aside and let me pass!" the woman snapped.

Ki peered around the edge of the rack, sure that Boston would not see him, absorbed as he was with the woman. The two were standing face to face, but as he watched, the woman stepped to one side to go around the big man. Boston stepped with her and grasped her wrist.

"Maybe you think I can't afford a fancy piece like you," he said. "Well, I got plenty of money. And plenty of what it takes to tickle you, too."

"Let go of me!" the woman said. "You're hurting my arm!"

"That ain't all I'll hurt if you don't open up!" Boston threatened. "If you'd rather go along with me now—"

Ki saw Boston's victim try to pull her arm free . Boston yanked it, almost pulling her off balance. She dropped her package and tried to push him away, but the big man grabbed her free arm and held it. Ki glanced at the counter and saw the clerk standing frozen, his eyes bulging, his mouth agape. Reluctantly he decided that he had no alternative. He stepped from behind the cutlery rack.

"Let the lady go," he commanded. "I'm not looking for more trouble with you, but if—"

Ki had no time to finish what he'd started to say. Boston tossed the woman aside and lunged for him.

Chapter 7

Ki was prepared for Boston's attack. He twisted his body to one side as the man reached him, and as Boston brushed past him, Ki loosed a knife-hand strike, the hard edge of his stiffened hand landing on the bandage that covered Boston's already injured nose.

Boston roared with anger and pain. His arms flailing wildly, he managed to grasp the fabric of Ki's jacket. Boston was falling at the time, but so great was his strength that, even while he fell, he swung Ki around by the hold he had on the jacket.

Ki tried to brace his feet, but Boston's weight and strength defied even his trained muscles. Ki could not stop himself. He saw that he was going to be thrown into the cutlery stand, and prepared himself for the impact. Then he went with the stand to the floor as it fell with a crash, sending the knives that it held in a scattering of bright, flashing steel as they sailed through the air and clattered to the floor.

Rolling away from Boston, Ki regained his feet with catlike quickness. Boston was slower in getting up, but when he came to his feet, he had a wicked-looking butcher knife in his right hand. For a split second, Ki's hand moved toward his *tanto*, but almost instantly reason conquered instinct; he didn't want to make himself yet more conspicuous by killing this evil-tempered plug-ugly.

Boston lunged, the knife held low in his hamlike fist. Ki shifted his weight to one foot and turned. As the knife

71

whispered past his belly, he reached out and, grasping Boston's wrist, gave it a quick outward twist with all the power that lay in the supple muscles of his arms.

The knife immediately fell to the floor, but Ki continued to twist Boston's arm. The man tried to pull free as Ki applied full pressure to the twist that was inexorably forcing the bone of his upper arm out of its shoulder socket, but Ki kept extending the arm as he twisted. As Boston bent forward to recover his balance and ease the pain of his tortured wrist and shoulder, Ki simply brought up his knee.

Again, his target was Boston's injured nose. The big man screamed as Ki's foot crashed into the bandage. The scream did not last long. It gurgled into silence as Boston lost consciousness, unable to stand the pain.

Ki let Boston's arm drop limply to the floor, and stepped over to the woman. The combat had lasted less than a minute, and she was still standing with her mouth agape, staring at Boston's hulking form where it lay quietly on the floor.

"Perhaps you'd better leave while he's still unconscious," Ki suggested, motioning toward the supine heap.

"You—you didn't kill him, did you?" she asked in a breathless whisper.

"Of course not. He's unconscious, but he'll be coming to in a few minutes."

"Then I—" The woman stopped and stared at Ki. "But you're hurt too!" she gasped. "You're bleeding!"

Ki's hand found the place on his cheek where her eyes were focused, and felt a trickle of warm wet blood. His cheek pained him when he ran his fingertips over the area where the blood was coming from.

"Here," she said. "Let me." Taking a handkerchief from her purse, she pressed it gently to the sore spot of his cheek. "It's not a big cut, but you can't just let it bleed."

"It'll be all right," Ki told her. "I've been cut before."

"Yes, but it needs to be tended to now," she insisted.

On the floor, Boston groaned and stirred. They looked down at the recumbent giant. His eyes were still closed and his head lay on the floor, but he was trying to move the arm that Ki had twisted.

"Please," the woman said, "I want to get out of here before that monster comes to and starts making trouble again. I live just a little way from here. If you don't mind walking home with me, I'll fix that cut for you. At least it'll save you the expense of going to a doctor."

Ki's first thought was to refuse, but the anxious look in the woman's dark brown eyes changed his mind. He nodded and said, "All right. Here, give me your package. I'll carry it and go with you."

Behind the counter, the clerk had not spoken nor stirred. Ki looked back and smiled inwardly when he saw the expression of relief that swept over the man's face as he and the woman walked out of the store. She took Ki's arm and led him along the street. After they'd gone a few steps, she looked up at him and smiled.

"You know, I haven't even thanked you for saving me from that brute back there in the store," she said.

"I don't need any thanks, Miss—"

"LaTour. Belle LaTour."

"I'm very pleased to meet you, Miss LaTour. My name is Ki."

"Ki? Ki what?"

"Just Ki. Nothing more."

"Ki," she repeated. "You look like you're Chinese, yet you don't."

"I'm not. I'm half Japanese, half American."

"Oh. I see." Belle LaTour's rising inflection made it clear that she didn't see, but that she was not going to ask any more questions. They reached an intersection and she pressed Ki's arm to guide him around the corner. After they'd walked a short distance in silence down the narrow deserted lane, past houses lighted in the early evening dark, she went on, "I hope you didn't believe I'm what that big ugly creature back there accused me of being. I'm not the kind of woman he took me for."

"I'm afraid his mind is as ugly as his face," Ki said.

"It certainly is! And he's got a mean temper too!"

"Don't blame yourself for the way he attacked me, Miss LaTour."

"Please call me Belle," she said. "It's friendlier. And I do feel like you're a friend, Ki."

"Thank you, Belle. As I was about to say, Boston and I had a little argument in a restaurant yesterday evening. That's why his face is bandaged."

"Boston is the brute's name?"

"Yes."

"And you got the best of him before?"

"Yes."

"Goodness! You sure must have big muscles," she said. She tightened her grip on Ki's forearm. "That fellow's twice as big as you, but you had him down on the floor before I knew what was happening."

"It's not having big muscles, Belle," Ki told her. "Knowing how to use the strength you have is what's important."

"Well, I'll say this much," she replied. "That's something you sure know how to do!"

"Practice," Ki said modestly. "That's the —"

He fell silent as Belle turned onto a brick walkway that led to a small house, set farther back from the street than its neighbors. Light glowed through a curtained window on one side, and Ki hesitated for a moment. Belle tugged his arm, and he followed her up the steps to the porch that ran across the front of the dwelling.

"Don't worry about the light being on," she said, taking a key from her handbag and unlocking the door. "There's not anybody inside. I leave a lamp burning when I go out. I—well, I don't like to go into a dark room all by myself."

Ki nodded as she swung the door open.

He followed her inside, and found himself in an entry-way. Doors were set into both short walls on the sides, as well as the one directly ahead. Belle opened one of the doors, and light flooded into the entry. She locked the front door, motioned to Ki to go into the lighted room, and followed him.

It was a crowded room, and the furniture in it was obviously expensive. An oblong bowlegged table occupied most of the space in the center, an oversized divan stood against the wall opposite the door, chairs had been placed in pairs against the front and inner walls, and a curio cabinet bulged out from the wall at the rear. In that wall a door stood ajar, giving Ki a glimpse of the corner of a kitchen table.

Belle pushed the door open and said, "I'll light the lamp in the kitchen. Just put that package on the table, while I stir up some permanganate."

Ki followed Belle into the kitchen and placed the package on the table. She took a bottle of purple crystals from a shallow cabinet that stood near the door, and a small bowl from a deeper one that occupied the wall beside the stove. A graniteware font hung on the opposite side of the room, and she drew water from it into the bowl.

As she returned to the table, her hand shook and a drop or two of water splashed from the bowl onto her skirt. She said, "Ki, sit down and wait just a minute. I don't dare spill any of this permanganate after I mix it. If it gets on my dress, it'll ruin it."

Obediently, suppressing his surprise and amusement, Ki sat on one of the kitchen chairs. After what seemed a very

75

long wait, Belle reappeared. She now wore a white satin dressing gown, and had taken off her hat. She looked different in other ways as well, not quite as stiffly erect as she had been, and her body seemed more flexible as well as more feminine. After watching her for a moment, Ki realized that she'd taken off her corset. As she came closer he got a whiff of freshly applied perfume, a heavy, sensuous scent.

"Now I can fix your face," she said, dribbling some of the permanganate crystals into the bowl of water and taking a spoon from a drawer to stir them.

"It really doesn't hurt now," Ki said.

"Just the same, it needs to be disinfected." She took a cloth from the table drawer and folded it across her arm.

"I don't think there's much danger of infection," Ki said. "Those knives were all new, they'd never been used before."

But Belle was not to be dissuaded. "Oh my!" she exclaimed. "Your jacket sleeve got cut somehow while you were scuffling with that brute!"

Ki twisted his arm and saw a rip an inch or so long near the cuff. He said, "That's all right. I have another jacket."

"It's not all right. Take it off, Ki. I'll mend it for you after I fix your face. After all, I'm responsible for that man attacking you."

Deciding that it would be easier to give in than to argue, Ki let the jacket slip off his shoulders. Belle dipped a corner of the rag in the permanganate solution, and started to reach out toward his cheek, then shook her head and pulled her hand back.

"What's wrong?" Ki asked.

"Well," she said, "I'm afraid I'll get this on your shirt."

"Don't worry about it," he told her.

"No, really," she said, "I think you should take it off."

Ki looked at her quizzically for a moment, then sighed

and undid his string tie, unbuttoned the shirt, and took it off, throwing it over the back of a kitchen chair.

Belle reached out with the permanganate-soaked rag, and daubed it on the cut. It stung, and Ki's muscles rippled involuntarily.

"My goodness! I thought you said you didn't have good muscles, Ki! But just look at you!"

Belle put her hand on Ki's shoulders and ran her fingers lightly down his arms. Ki looked at her face. Her eyes were half closed and her lips were parted sensuously as she stroked his smooth skin.

"Belle," he said quietly. "Do you know what you're doing?"

"Yes. I know what I'm doing, but I can't help myself."

Belle's arms suddenly went around Ki's chest and she pulled him to her in a firm embrace. He could feel the warmth of her soft body as she held herself against him. He took her wrists and gently broke the embrace.

"Perhaps I'd better go," he said, reaching for his jacket. "I'll get the rip sewn up later. Thank you for taking care of my face, Belle."

"Wait, Ki," she said. "I know why you're going. You think I lied to you about not being a—well, a fallen woman."

"To tell you the truth, I don't quite know what to think."

"I know what you're likely thinking right now," she said in a subdued voice. "You're thinking that big fellow was right. Well, he wasn't! But that doesn't keep me from needing a man. Please stay with me, even just a little while."

"You're not married, then?"

"Do I look like I am?"

"Nobody can tell whether a woman's married just by looking at her," Ki said.

"Look." Belle extended both her hands. On her left ring finger there was a gold-set cameo, and on her right hand

77

she wore a ring set with a ruby or a garnet, he could not tell which at a glance. "Don't you think I'd be wearing a wedding ring if I had a husband?"

"Yes, I suppose you would, Belle. But this house—"

"You act like you never heard of a widow, Ki."

"I suppose I didn't think of you as a widow because you're so young."

"Then you'll—"

"Yes. If you want me to."

Belle sighed and stepped up close to him. Again he caught the fragrance of her musky perfume as she lifted her arms and ran her hands down his arms from his shoulders, lingeringly caressing his biceps. Ki held her to him, and now the warm softness of her full breasts aroused him. Belle's hands were traveling over Ki's bare back and arms, and he bent to kiss her neck. Belle quivered as his warm lips pushed aside the collar of her gown and moved down her soft, perfumed shoulders.

"No more in here, Ki," she gasped. She found Ki's hand and led him toward the door on the far side of the kitchen, saying, "The bedroom's this way."

Light from the kitchen lamp spilled softly through the open door. As his eyes adjusted to the dimness, Ki saw a wide bed across the room, and, in the shadowed areas of the walls, the dark shapes of a bureau and chairs and a wash stand. He gave little attention to his surroundings, for Belle's hands were in constant motion, stroking his chest and occasionally stealing down to his groin.

Belle stopped before they reached the bed and began fumbling at the waistband of his trousers. He was aware of her soft hands brushing down his hips while he slipped her gown off her shoulders and saw the dark tips of her full soft breasts inviting his lips. He bent to kiss them, and Belle sighed, but did not interrupt the exploration of his body with her busy fingers.

He found the knot in the sash of her dressing gown and pulled it free. The white robe slipped off and Ki ran his hand down the gentle swell of Belle's stomach, feeling it contract and quiver under his touch. Then he lifted her and carried her to the bed, and lay her gently down upon it. She reached out with an eager hand and stroked the swelling at the front of his trousers.

"Oh my!" she whispered, an urgent quaver in her voice. "Take off your clothes, Ki! Hurry!"

He quickly took off his boots and trousers, and moved toward the bed. Belle lay back, spreading her thighs wide and reaching out for him. As he climbed on the bed and poised himself above her, she slipped a hand around his rock-hard shaft and guided him into her moist, enfolding warmth.

Belle cried out, a low-pitched sigh of pleasure as Ki filled her. She clasped his hips and pulled him to her and whispered, "Oh, Ki! Don't move for a minute, please! I just want to feel you filling me! I've been empty too long!"

Ki held himself pressed to her until he felt her stirring, then he began to move. Belle responded eagerly. She rolled her hips from side to side, soft moans of ecstasy bubbling from her throat. As Ki kept up his steady lunges, the moans grew higher-pitched and shorter. Her body began quivering, and the motion of her hips sped up under Ki's steady thrusts, until she was writhing constantly.

Ki did not change his tempo. He drove steadily and hard until a scream burst from Belle's throat. She bounced and tossed beneath him until the scream faded to a soft whimper and her body grew still. When he did not slow the speed or vigor of his movement, Belle stirred and sighed.

"My God!" she gasped. "You're still as big and hard as ever! How much longer can you keep this up?"

"Enjoyment is all the greater when it is prolonged," he said. "But if you're tired—"

"No, no!" she replied quickly. "I don't want you to stop yet. Not for a long time!"

Ki did not stop, but merely slowed the tempo of his thrusts. He moved more deliberately, sinking into Belle's receptive body and holding himself pressed firmly against her yielding flesh for several moments at the end of each prolonged stroke. Belle lay quiet for only a short time, her eyes tightly closed. Then she began to twist her hips once more, rising to meet Ki's deep lunges. Her eyes opened and her breath started gusting.

"Will you come with me this time, Ki?" she asked.

"Would it please you if I did?"

"Nothing could please me more than what you're doing right now. But how long can you keep it up?"

"Until I choose to stop. Unless you—"

"I'm not going to ask you to stop," Belle broke in. "You're the kind of man a woman dreams about. Keep going as long as you want to, and I'll stay right with you."

"That will be good," Ki replied. "Pleasure shared is twice delightful."

"Oh yes," Belle sighed. "And I'm just about to have some more pleasure, Ki. Just go on doing what you are right now."

Gradually he increased his rhythm for a short while, then her breathing became faster and her undulations more frantic. Her gentle sighs mounted to sharp, small screams, and when he felt her body begin to jerk in her orgasm, he stopped with his shaft buried to its full length, while her hips jerked and her back arched and her cries peaked and died away.

This time he gave her no respite, but started driving again as soon as she began to grow quiet. She gave a long, throaty moan of pleasure mixed with pain, but she did not protest. As Ki continued his steady stroking, she clamped her legs around him again, her knees spread to open her thighs wider, and rose to meet each thrust.

Ki released his control as Belle's movements grew more and more frantic. He built to his long-delayed climax while her sobs of pleasure filled the small room. Her long blond hair was loose now, and spread across the pillow. Her eyes were squeezed shut and her full lips were clamped together as she went into the final moments of her spasm. Her hips were jerking up and down frantically now, and she no longer matched Ki's steady rhythm.

As he neared his climax, he went into Belle's willing body even deeper than before, holding back now only until she began her final, frenzied burst of twisting, writhing, jerky bounces, her mind no longer in control of her body. Then Ki surrendered his control, too. His hips worked up and down in a short burst of rhythmless staccato thrusts until he was completely drained. Only then did he relax and let his muscular body sag onto Belle's soft flesh, while both of them lay quiet and spent.

Chapter 8

Jessie woke with a start in her bed in the Miner's Rest, and, with a reaction that was almost instinctive, reached for the Colt that was under her pillow. She moved her arm quietly, her eyes searching the room's darkness as her hand closed around the pistol's peachwood grips.

She was sure that something had awakened her, but was not yet certain what it had been. She lay still, listening to the night. She heard nothing, and decided she must have been dreaming. She was settling down to go back to sleep when the silence was broken.

"I don't mean you any harm, Miss Starbuck," a strange voice said from somewhere past the footboard of her bed. "I'm sure you took a gun from under your pillow, but I hope I can persuade you not to use it."

Jessie did not answer at once. The voice puzzled her; it was neither male nor female, but had overtones of each. It was high-pitched and slightly hoarse, obviously disguised, and she could not locate its source. She looked quickly around the room again, and though her eyes had now been open long enough to adjust to the almost pitch blackness of the room, she had not been able to locate its source.

"Let me suggest that if I'd planned to harm you, I had all the opportunity I needed before you awoke," the strange voice went on. "Think about that before you think about the gun I'm sure you must have in your hand by now."

Again, Jessie held back from answering. She was sure

she'd located the spot from which the voice was coming, for the only place of concealment was on the other side of a wardrobe standing against the wall that ran at right angles to the bed. However, when she thought of what her mysterious visitor had said, she was forced to agree with the logic of the statement.

"All right," she said at last. "You've convinced me that you're not here for any reason except to talk. Go ahead and have your say. I won't shoot, at least not now."

"Your decision does credit to your wisdom, Miss Starbuck," the strange-toned voice replied. "When you've heard what I have to tell you, you'll be glad you listened."

Jessie was still trying to analyze the voice, but could get no clue from it as to the mysterious intruder's name or sex. She saw a shapeless figure emerge from behind the wardrobe. Peering through the darkness, she decided that the midnight visitor was draped in a blanket. Although she felt easier in her mind now about her caller's purpose, she shifted the muzzle of the Colt to cover the shapeless figure.

"Before you give me your message, whatever it is," Jessie said, "I hope you'll answer a question or two."

"What are they?"

"One is why you felt it was necessary to make such a mystery of your visit," she replied. "The other is how you managed to get in here without disturbing me."

Jessie strained her ears, anticipating the reply, hoping she'd get a clue that would help her identify her visitor.

"I'm afraid I can't answer either question," the disguised voice croaked. "But you will know the answer in due time."

"I certainly hope so!" Jessie replied. She went on, "What do you have to tell me that's important enough for you to take such a strange way of saying it?"

"Do you consider the Starbuck mines important?"

"Of course I do! If I didn't, I wouldn't be here!"

"Then move very carefully, Miss Starbuck. Your mines are in great danger."

"What kind of danger?"

"Danger from within, danger from without."

"Can't you tell me something more specific?"

"You will find out, if you look carefully enough."

"Where do I start looking?"

"Look everywhere, Miss Starbuck! Everywhere!"

"How long do I have to look?"

"Very little time. Do not waste a day, or even an hour."

"Can't you tell me what kind of danger to look for?"

"If you look carefully, you will find it."

"And you can't tell me anything more?"

"No. The rest is up to you and your companion."

"Ki? Is he in danger too?"

"As much as you yourself." The hidden speaker began moving toward the door. "That is all I can tell you, Miss Starbuck. Please do not take my message lightly!"

Jessie had planned to get some idea of the stranger's identity when he or she went into the hall. She heard the door latch grate, but the expected rectangle of light did not appear. The passageway was darker than the room, and the draped figure had already disappeared into the blackness.

Jessie realized then that the mysterious intruder must have blown out the night light that had been burning in the hall. She got up, found her deduction was correct, and locked the door. Back in bed, she sank down and replaced her gun under the pillow. She lay quietly, thinking about the strange visitor until she fell asleep again.

"I had a strange visitor last night," Jessie told Ki as she opened the door to his tapping the next morning. "I hoped you'd hear us talking, but you must have been sleeping so soundly that we didn't disturb you."

84

"I'm afraid I wasn't there to hear you," Ki said. "I just got back to my room an hour or so ago."

Jessie saw the strip of sticking plaster on his cheek then. With a puzzled frown, she asked, "Trouble?"

"Nothing to be alarmed about. I went into a store to ask where the Oriental quarter is, and ran into Boston again."

"And that kept you out until an hour ago?"

"There's a little bit more to it. Let's talk about it at breakfast. If you're ready—"

"Of course I am, I was waiting for you." As they walked down the hall she went on, "Either Fred Edmonds has told someone we're here, Ki, or someone at Starhope recognized me yesterday. Whoever that was in my room last night called me by name."

"Perhaps it's just as well that you'd already decided to drop your reporter pose."

"It wasn't a very good idea to begin with."

They reached the dining room and sat down. The waiter came to their table and poured coffee, then went to get their food. The hotel had no menus; its guests ate whatever the cook decided to prepare.

Ki said, "Tell me about your mysterious visitor. I hope he didn't give you any trouble."

"No. But I don't know whether it was a man or a woman, Ki. That's the biggest mystery of all, to me."

"What was the threat?"

"It wasn't a threat, but a warning that we're in some kind of danger here, and that the mines are too."

"Danger of what, Jessie?"

"He didn't say. His—" Jessie stopped short and shook her head. "I think of whoever it was as 'he,' but the voice could have been either a man's or a woman's. Whoever it was said the danger is from within and without."

"Nothing more than that?"

Jessie shook her head as the waiter came back with their breakfasts. He placed on the table a plate stacked with pancakes, a bowl of scrambled eggs, and a platter of thinly sliced ham, added a pitcher of syrup and a pot of jam, and returned to the kitchen. Jessie served herself, passing the service dishes to Ki. When their plates had been filled, she picked up her story.

"What happened last night was very mysterious. My caller managed to get into my room, even though I'd locked the door. He'd blown out the night light in the hall, and was draped in a blanket, or something like that, which covered him entirely."

"It must be someone you know, Jessie," Ki said, frowning.

"I think so too, even if the voice wasn't familiar. It was high-pitched and muffled, and I'm sure purposely distorted. Of course, I thought at once that it must be someone from the mines, or from Starhope, since Fred Edmonds is the only one who knows we're in Copperopolis. But I can't say it was Edmonds's voice."

"And he called you by name?"

"Yes. Always 'Miss Starbuck,' Never 'Jessie.' Very formal and polite, but it's certainly started me to wondering."

"Perhaps we'll get a clue today. You are planning to go to the mines, aren't you?"

"Yes. I intend to do a great deal of close looking, Ki."

"Well, the clue's out there somewhere," he said.

"I'm sure it is. Now tell me what happened between you and Boston. You must've fought again, judging by your face."

"Boston didn't do that, Jessie, at least not intentionally. I fell against a rack of cutlery in the store, and one of the knives nicked me when the rack toppled over."

"How did you happen to get into another fight with him?"

86

"He came into the store while I was there, waiting for the clerk to complete a sale to a young lady. Boston began tormenting the girl, and I felt that I had to stop him."

"I'm sure you did," Jessie said dryly.

Ignoring the smile in Jessie's voice, Ki went on, "There's not much to tell. He came at me with a knife, and I disarmed him and knocked him out. The lady insisted that I go home with her so she could tend to my cut. That's about all."

"I see." Jessie's voice was expressionless.

There was a long-standing, unspoken agreement between her and Ki that their private affairs would never be discussed and that neither one would question the other. What they did when they were apart could just as well have happened to other people in another world. The agreement had worked out so well that neither was of a mind to change it.

They had been eating while they talked, and now Ki pushed his plate away. Jessie took a last bite of syrup-laden hotcakes, swallowed the coffee that remained in her cup, wiped her lips with her napkin, and stood up.

"Shall we start for the mines?" she asked. "I'm curious to see what we're going to find out."

"Miss Starbuck!" Fred Edmonds exclaimed when Jessie and Ki walked into the rambling building that housed the mine offices. "What a pleasant surprise to see you here!"

"Thank you, Mr. Edmonds."

Jessie glanced around the big, high-ceilinged room. It had changed little since her last visit. There were the same desks, the same rows of file cases, the same cabinets with their small metal-lined drawers to hold ore samples, and the same tables piled high with files and reports. The hat rack on one side of the door and the gun rack on the other, the latter containing two rifles and two shotguns, were also just as they'd been on earlier visits.

She did not recognize the young man who sat at a desk far back in one corner, but the bent, wrinkled gray-head who was standing beside a wide desk under a bank of windows was a man she'd known for many years. He came to her, his hand extended.

"Little Jessie!" he exclaimed. Then, as Jessie took his hand in both of hers, he added, "I guess I still think of you that way, Jessie. But it's 'Miss Starbuck' now, all right."

"I'll always be Jessie to you, Mr. McKelway," she smiled. "And of course, you remember Ki."

"Indeed I do," McKelway replied.

"You look very good," Jessie said to the oldster. "I think living in Copperopolis agrees with you."

"It does, now that I'm used to it," McKelway replied. "Are you going to be here long, Jessie?"

"For a while. There are some things I need to look at, a lot of reports to go over. And I wanted to go into the mines and take a look at them, as well. You'll probably be tired of having me in your way before I get everything done."

Edmonds broke in to say, "I don't think you've met Eric Johanssen, Miss Starbuck. He's only been working here a little more than two years."

Jessie extended her hand to the young man who'd come up from his desk in the back to join the group. "Eric," she said. "I hope you're happy working here?"

"Oh yes, Miss Starbuck," he answered. "I'm learning about mining in a way my father never had a chance to. He used to work in the stopes, before he was killed in a train wreck."

"And Mr. Mason gave you a job?" Jessie asked.

"Yes, he did. And in the office too."

"Where is Mr. Mason, by the way?" Jessie asked.

"He's in Virginia City, Miss Starbuck," Edmonds replied. "He should be back tomorrow, or the next day at the latest. But if you're in a hurry, there's no need for you to wait for him to get back. We can help you get started with what you plan to do."

"I think the first thing I want to do is get settled in the company flat here at the mine. Since I'm going to be working in the office here, there's no point in our wasting time traveling to and from Copperopolis every day."

"It's all ready for you to move into, Miss Starbuck," young Johanssen volunteered. "Keeping it tidy is one of my jobs."

"Good. We'll get settled, and then I'll come down and see what else I'm going to need you to help me with," Jessie said. "Come on, Ki. Let's get our bags from the buggy."

"I'll go and unlock the door and turn on the water valve from the cistern," Eric said. "Then, if you see anything else I can do, I'll be there handy."

Alex Starbuck had built the present office building before the town of Copperopolis existed. Although he was accustomed to rough accommodations, he'd seen no point being uncomfortable when visiting his property. He'd added a suite of two bedrooms, a sitting room that he used as an office, a compact kitchen, and a bathroom to the building's plans.

Jessie had used the suite only once since her father's death, but now she was glad to be able to enjoy both comfort and privacy. Ki carried their bags upstairs while young Eric Johanssen turned on the valve that allowed water from the cistern on the roof to flow into the suite's pipes. After he'd turned it on and tested it, and shown Jessie where the can of coal oil for the lamps and the kitchen range was kept, he stood looking at her as though awaiting further instructions.

"Thank you, Eric, I think that's all I need to know," she

told him. "But I'll need your help again, later, when I come down to begin looking through the office files."

When the youth had gone, Jessie said, "We overlooked one thing, Ki, in our hurry to get started."

"Yes, I realized that while I was getting the bags. We have a kitchen, but nothing to cook."

"While I'm working on the files, why don't you go into town and get what we need to stock the kitchen for a few days?" Jessie suggested.

"If you don't mind having a late lunch," Ki said. "Even if I leave right now, I can't be back by noon."

"After that big breakfast we had, putting off lunch an hour or so won't bother me a bit. There's still a lot of the morning left, and I don't see any reason to wait until afternoon to start checking them. And the sooner I wind up this problem here, the sooner we can get back to the Circle Star."

With Ki on his way to town, Jessie went into the office. Edmonds came to the door to greet her, and pointed to a desk at the rear of the barnlike room.

"We've cleared that desk for you," Miss Starbuck," he said. "I suppose you're down here to start?"

"Yes. But I don't want to interrupt your work," Jessie replied. "If you'll just refresh my memory about the files, I can probably find everything I need. But before I do anything else, I want to know how much trouble Saul Goodwin and the Knights of Labor have been giving you."

There was a moment of silence as Edmonds, McKelway, and young Johanssen exchanged glances, then McKelway said, "They don't bother us here in the office, Jessie. Underground, now, in the stopes, that's another matter."

"Mac is right," Edmonds agreed. "The three of us here in the office don't interest them. They're after the five hundred men in the three main shafts."

90

"Are they signing up many members?" Jessie asked.

Edmonds shrugged. "Who knows? The men who sign up don't talk about it, and the ones who don't sign up just go about their work as though Goodwin and his enforcers didn't even exist."

"Two of our men have quit. They're enforcers for Goodwin now," Johanssen volunteered. "They were at Starhope about a week ago, to talk to some of the men while they were at home. A bunch of the others heard they were there and chased them off."

"Is that the only trouble we've had?" Jessie asked.

"It's the only trouble we know about," McKelway said, after Edmonds did not reply at once. "Lord only knows how many little fistfights there've been underground, or in town."

"If you hear anything about Goodwin or his men, I want to know it at once," Jessie told them. "Now, if you'll show me how the cabinets are marked, I'll get busy with the files."

Ki finished his shopping without wasting time, and loaded his purchases in the buggy. He was climbing into the seat when he remembered he'd promised Belle that he'd visit her again this evening. Leaving the buggy at the hitch rail, he walked the short distance to her house and tapped at the door.

"Ki!" Belle exclaimed when she saw him. Her face looked pale without the rouge, and her lips were thinner than he remembered. She was wearing the same white robe she'd been wearing the previous night, and her blond hair was tousled. "I didn't expect you until evening. You ought to warn a girl before you knock at her door in the morning, when she's not expecting you. I must look terrible!"

"You look very good to me," Ki said.

"Well, come inside before we give the neighbors something to gossip about," Belle told him. "Not that they won't anyhow."

Inside the house, Belle took Ki's hand and led him to the bedroom before he had a chance to protest. She threw her arms around him and turned her lips up to be kissed.

Ki bent to meet them with his, and as their tongues entwined he felt Belle's hand slide between their bodies. She broke off their kiss and took a half-step back, shrugged her shoulders, and let her robe slide to the floor. She wore nothing under it. Her skin glowed in the soft light filtering through the drawn shades, and the pink nipples of her full breasts protruded from their darker pink rosettes.

Ki said quickly, "Belle, I'd like to start where we left off last night, but I can't stay."

"Not even a little while?" Belle asked persuasively. "It's always better in the morning when I first get up."

"No, Belle," Ki broke in, his voice firm. "I just stopped by to tell you that I might not get back to town tonight."

"You're not leaving for good, are you?"

"No. But we're—"

A sharp staccato knocking at the front door interrupted Ki. He looked questioningly at Belle. She rushed to the window and pulled the blind aside a crack to peer out.

"Oh my God!" she exclaimed. "It's Jared! Ki, you've got to go out the back way. I can't explain now, but I can't let the man at the door find you here. Just go out quietly through the kitchen, and I'll explain everything the next time I see you."

Picking up her robe and donning it as she went out, Belle left quickly. Ki stood motionless. The name Jared had rung a bell in his mind. It was an unusual name, and the only man in Copperopolis likely to bear it was Jared Mason, the general superintendent of the Starbuck mines.

Walking quietly, Ki went into the kitchen. Belle had shut

the connecting door into the living room, and he cracked it open an unnoticeable hair's breadth. Standing stock-still, Ki waited.

Chapter 9

Because of the position in which he was forced to stand, Ki could not see into the living room, but as Mason and Belle came into the room he could hear them plainly. Mason was talking.

"But before I go out to the office," he was saying, "I need to talk to Saul. Run and tell him I'm back, and that I want him to come over here right away."

"Just as soon as I slip on a dress," Belle replied.

"To hell with a dress!" Mason snapped. "I'm in a hurry, and nobody'll notice you going through the backyard. Go on, do as I say!"

Ki barely had time to beat a silent retreat into the bedroom before Belle came through the kitchen and went out the back door. Now he could only watch by going into the hall, but he decided that would be too risky. He settled down and waited for Belle to return with the Knights of Labor organizer.

Belle returned alone. "Mr. Goodwin's not home," she told Mason. "I knocked and knocked, but nobody answered the door."

"Damn it!" Mason snapped. "I need to know what the hell he did while I was gone."

"Well, I can tell you something one of his men did!" Belle said angrily. "That big fellow—"

"Shut up, Belle," Mason commanded. "You can tell me about it some other time. If Saul's not there, I'll just have to talk to him later. Right now I've got to get out to the mine."

"You mean you're not going to stay with me awhile?"

"Not right now. Look for me tonight, though."

"Don't I always?" she asked. There was no reply; Ki only heard the slamming of the front door as Mason left.

As soon as he was sure Mason had gone, Ki stepped into the living room. Belle was sitting in one of the armchairs, her jaw clenched, an unhappy scowl on her face. Her eyes grew wide when she saw him.

"You—you didn't go, like I told you to!" she gasped.

"No. I decided I'd better know exactly what your situation is, Belle. You didn't tell me last night that you had a—well, let's say a protector."

"I guess I lied to you, Ki. I didn't mean any harm by it, though. I was lonesome and—well, I just wanted to have a real man for a change."

"Jared Mason is not a satisfactory lover?" Ki asked.

"He's not worth—" Belle stopped suddenly. Her eyes narrowed and she went on, "You haven't any right to ask me that kind of a question, any more than you've a right to snoop around and listen to what Jared and I said!"

"Perhaps not," Ki admitted. "I stayed because I thought you and Jared Mason might say something interesting, and as it happens, you did."

Belle's eyes narrowed suspiciously. "You know Jared?" she asked.

"Not as well as you do, Belle. As it happens, Mason and I work for the same employer. I'm sure you've heard of her. Her name is Jessie Starbuck."

"Oh my God!" Belle gasped. "What kind of trouble have I got into now! If Jared finds out about you and me—"

Ki interrupted her. "You won't be in any trouble at all, if you give me a little help."

"What kind of help?"

"Tell me what's going on between Mason and Saul Goodwin."

"I can't do that, Ki!" she protested. "If Jared found out about it, he'd tell Goodwin. And that Goodwin's a mean man. He wouldn't think twice about turning me over to his enforcers, and that'd be the last anybody ever heard or saw of me."

"You seem to know a lot about Goodwin, Belle."

"All I know is what I've heard him and Jared talking about, when they get together here."

"Do they use your house as a regular meeting place?"

"It's not really my house, Ki. I lied about that too. It's Jared's."

"Was it Mason's idea for you to invite me here?"

"No!" Belle protested. "He didn't have anything to do with it! I knew he wouldn't be back from Virginia City for a day or two, and after I'd seen you handle that big brute in the store, I got the idea I'd like to—well, you know, Ki. A girl can stand a played-out old coot like Jared just so long, and then she's got to have a real man for a change."

"Then you didn't know Boston is one of Goodwin's enforcers?"

She gasped and buried her head in her hands. "I swear I didn't, Ki!"

Belle's protest rang true. Ki believed her, but he did not let up in his questioning. He asked, "How often do Mason and Goodwin meet here?"

"It all depends. Sometimes they'll talk every few days, then maybe it'll be two or three weeks before they get together."

"Have you heard them talking about the Starbuck mines?"

"Oh yes. The Starbuck and the Anaconda both."

"Do they just talk about the Knights of Labor, or do they talk about other things as well?"

"Ki, I don't listen carefully to what they say; I'm not all that curious. Sometimes I'm not even in the parlor while they're talking."

An idea had been taking shape in Ki's mind. It was not one that appealed to him, but he could see no other way to get the information Jessie needed. He asked Belle, "When do they usually get together?"

"Nights, mostly. After supper. I never know when Jared's coming to see me. Except tonight, you heard him say he'd be back. He's got some way of getting word to Goodwin when he wants to meet him here, so I guess Goodwin will be here too."

"Belle," he asked carefully, "how would you feel about helping me hear what Mason and Goodwin talk about tonight?"

She did not answer for several moments, then she said, "I don't know. Help you how?"

"Hide me so I can hear what Mason and Goodwin talk about."

This time she was silent even longer. At last she replied. "Don't ask me to do that, Ki! Jared might not be such a much, but he's all I've got."

"Mason will never know about it, Belle, I promise you that. And if I know what his plans are, I might be able to stop him from getting into really serious trouble later on."

"What kind of trouble? Is Jared doing something crooked?"

"He might not have done anything against the law up to now, but if I'm right, he's about to."

"And you think you can stop him?"

"I'd like to stop him. Not because I care anything about Mason, but because what he's planning can hurt Jessie Star-buck."

"She's the one that owns the Starbuck mines, isn't she? I guess you'd call her Jared's boss?"

"Yes. She's my boss too, Belle."

"I've heard Jared talk about her, but I thought she lived someplace back East, or in Texas or somewhere."

"She has a ranch in Texas that's as much her home as anyplace. But let's not waste time talking about other things. I need to know what Mason and Goodwin are planning. Will you let me hide here when they meet tonight?"

"You're sure it'll help Jared stay out of trouble?"

"I think he's in trouble now. But if I know what he's up to with Goodwin, it's something that could put him in a jail cell for a long, long time."

Belle said, "I'd be out in the cold if that happened, wouldn't I?"

"Yes, of course you would."

"But if I said yes, where would you hide, Ki? There's no place I can think of that would do."

"Does this house have an attic?"

"I guess so. But if it does, I never have been up in it."

"That doesn't matter, as long as there's a trapdoor in one of the rooms that I can use to get into it."

"There's some kind of square frame in the pantry ceiling," Belle said, frowning thoughtfully. "Is that what you mean?"

"Probably. I'll go look."

Ki glanced at the pantry ceiling, got a chair from the kitchen, and placed it under the frame square. Standing on the chair, he pushed on the center of the framed area. The door was of the simplest construction, boards nailed to a cleat to make a square that rested on the frame of the opening. When Ki pushed, the door popped up and he shoved it aside. He could see the slanting rafters that supported the low-pitched roof. There was very little clearance between the rafters and the ceiling joists, but he was sure he could squeeze in. He replaced the trapdoor and jumped to the floor.

"I'll come back right after dark," he told Belle. "If Mason is here, leave a light in your bedroom and have the shade down. If he's not here, leave the shade up."

"Ki, what's Jared going to do to me if he catches you up there?" she asked, apprehension in her voice.

"He won't catch me, so don't worry. If he does, I can take care of him. You saw what happened to Boston."

Belle nodded slowly, but the worried frown did not leave her face. She asked, "What if he's got a gun?"

"Boston had a knife," Ki reminded her.

"That's not the same thing, Ki."

"Don't worry," Ki repeated. "I'll handle it if Mason finds out I'm up there. And you won't have to be involved. You can tell him I must've sneaked in while you were at the store or something."

"I can, can't I?" For the first time, Belle smiled. "All right, Ki. I'll remember about the bedroom light and the shade."

Ki wasted no time getting back to the livery stable. While the liveryman was getting the buggy, Ki remembered that Jessie might need her own transportation, and rented a horse as well as the buggy. He set out for the mines, leading the saddle horse behind the buggy.

Jessie was still in the office, going through records of the mines' past production and trying to reconcile them with operations statements and financial reports.

"But there are some things in them that don't make sense," she told him as they sat in the upstairs flat, eating a cold lunch. "Somebody's been juggling the figures that were sent to me at the Circle Star."

"There's only one person in a position to do that," Ki said thoughtfully.

"Yes. Jared Mason. I hate to think about it, because Alex

99

trusted him completely, and of course I did too."

"Mason will be here sometime within the next few hours, Jessie. He got back from Virginia City on the morning train."

"You've talked to him?"

"No. I listened to him. The first thing he did was try to get hold of Saul Goodwin."

"Goodwin!" she exclaimed, her eyes widening.

"Yes. To me, that means the two of them are in some sort of plot together."

"How did you find out about all this?"

"It's a long story, and I'd just as soon tell you about it later, if you don't mind waiting."

Jessie looked at him for a moment, studying his bland face. She nodded and said, "If you say so. But where do the Knights of Labor come into it?"

"I can think of two or three ways. So can you, now that you know what's been going on. But there's no use wasting our time just guessing, because if a plan I have works out, I'll be able to listen to Mason and Goodwin talking about their plans this evening."

"Ki, you're risking your life if they catch you!"

"They won't, if my plan works. And I'm sure it will."

"Just what are you going to do?"

"I know where they're meeting. There's only one reason for them to get together, and that's to talk over their plans. I'll hide and listen to them."

"I don't like the idea, Ki. It's dangerous."

"Has that ever stopped either of us before?"

She was silent for a moment, then she looked across the table at him and smiled. "No. And I can't argue with you about your scheme. If we know what Jared and Goodwin are planning, we can certainly keep a jump ahead of them. If we give Jared enough rope, I have an idea he'll hang himself."

100

"There's one thing I'd like for you to do, Jessie," Ki said. "Keep Mason here at the mines as late as possible."

"That certainly won't be hard to do," she said. "There are a lot of things I want to talk to him about."

"I'll be on my way back to town, then." Ki pushed his chair away from the table. "Don't worry if I'm late, Jessie. I hope I'll be able to follow Goodwin when he and Mason get through with whatever they'll be talking about."

"Good luck, Ki," Jessie said, then added, "So far, your luck's been a lot better than mine."

Leaving the buggy for Jessie, Ki mounted the saddle horse and started back to town. Although he did not think it likely that he'd encounter Mason on the rough trail, he took to the even rougher terrain away from the rutted road and came within sight of Copperopolis an hour or so before sundown. Dismounting, Ki tethered the horse, sat down cross-legged under one of the stunted pines, and waited patiently for darkness.

Mason arrived at the mines in midafternoon. He saw Jessie at the paper-strewn desk in the back of the office, and his jaw dropped for a moment before he regained his composure.

"Jessie!" he exclaimed. "What a pleasant surprise! I had no idea you were planning to visit us!"

"I didn't plan to, Jared," she replied, standing up to take his extended hand as he came to the desk. "It was just a spur-of-the-moment decision."

"I'm sorry I wasn't here to greet you," Mason said. "You should have wired me. I'd have put off my trip to Virginia City if I'd known you were going to be here."

"I wasn't exactly sure when I'd get here. We had some stops to make on the way."

"'We'?" Mason looked around the office. "Of course, Ki's with you. But where is he?"

"Off on some errands at the moment."

"Well, come into my office, where we can talk," Mason said. He looked at the others, who'd stopped work when he came in. "Is there anything urgent that we should talk about, Fred?" he asked Edmonds.

"Not a thing that won't wait, Mr. Mason," Edmonds replied. "Whenever you have time, I'll give you a report."

In Mason's office, he pulled a chair for Jessie up to his wide desk and settled into his own high-backed chair behind it. Jessie looked at Mason, keeping her face expressionless as she noted the changes in him since her last visit. The mine superintendent's hair was gray, his once thin and craggy face now puffed and florid, his body no longer trim, but bloated and soft.

"I suppose you're wondering about the figures on the statements for the last quarter," he said. "They weren't as good as I'd have liked."

"They weren't as good as they have been," Jessie agreed. "What's wrong, Jared?"

"I've had to close some of the stopes, Jessie. The ore out of them just isn't as rich as it was a year ago."

"But isn't that normal? My father told me that copper mining is just a matter of keeping the main tunnel pushed far enough ahead of the working stopes so that no time is wasted in opening new ones when the older ones begin to fall off."

"We may be coming to the end of the lode," Mason replied. "In Number One, we're at eighteen hundred feet, Number Two's at fourteen hundred, and Number Three is just past a thousand. And the reports from Anaconda show that we're getting more gangue and less copper in every ton. But you know that, of course, if you've seen the smelter figures."

"I haven't, Jared. Somehow the smelter reports were left out of the material you sent me."

"Why, that doesn't seem possible!" Mason said. "McKelway must have overlooked them; I'll have a talk to him about that. He's getting a bit old, Jessie. I don't want to let him go—"

"And I certainly wouldn't want you to," Jessie interrupted. "If he's made a mistake, we can overlook it. I'm sure you have copies of the smelter figures."

"Of course. I'll get them out for you tomorrow." Mason sat silent for a moment, then went on, "As I just said, we might be coming to the end of the lode. We can open a new shaft, which will be expensive. It means adding a lot more men, some new equipment. And there's no guarantee that a fourth shaft will increase production enough to make the expense profitable."

"What other choice have we?" Jessie asked.

"Have you ever thought of selling? I haven't discussed it with Daly, but I know the Anaconda would make a good offer. And there are other buyers around, if you feel like looking."

For a moment Jessie was silent, then she said, "Jared, my father didn't accomplish what he did by selling out or retreating from a challenge. Alex would have done whatever was necessary to keep the Starbuck mines moving ahead. And I certainly don't propose to do anything less."

For a moment, Mason did not reply. Then he said, "I agree with you about Alex, Jessie. And since you're his daughter, I certainly don't question your ability. But men look at these things differently than a woman might. I was just suggesting—"

"Being a woman doesn't cloud my judgment, Jared, any more that it would make me forget what Alex taught me."

"I wasn't hinting at either one," Mason said hastily. "But I'm closer to this situation than you are, Jessie. Things are changing here in Montana."

"Suppose you bring me up to date, then."

"For one thing, we'd really be in a bad situation if Marcus Daly decided he wanted to add the Starbuck mines to what he and Hearst already have at the Anaconda. All he'd need to do is tell us that he wouldn't smelt our ore any longer."

"Then we'd build our own smelter," Jessie said calmly. "If you remember, that was something Alex had planned to do. Daly offered to smelt for us at the Anaconda because he didn't have enough ore to keep the smelter busy 'round the clock."

"He has now, I'm sure," Mason said.

"Then if he decides to stop smelting Starbuck ore, we'll go ahead and build our own smelter."

"We could do that, of course, but it'd be very expensive. Don't underrate Daly, Jessie. He's become a real power here in Montana. I heard something in Virginia City that should interest you. Daly's been trying to get the state capital moved to Copperopolis. I understand he's got almost enough political backing to do it now."

"If he's planning something of that kind, he's going to be too busy to spend much time worrying about us, Jared," Jessie said calmly. "What else do you think I've overlooked, or haven't heard about?"

"I suppose you've heard about the Knights of Labor?"

"A little bit. Not as much as I'll hear before I leave, I'm sure. But there've always been unsatisfied workmen. As far as I can see, there always will be."

"If they get enough of our men signed up, we could be in trouble. Suppose the men in the mine ask for more money?"

"Then we'll talk to them and see if we can't agree on something less than they hope to get, and settle for something we can afford to pay. I won't squeeze an extra penny or two of profit out of the men who do the work, Jared."

"What if they walk out of the mine?"

"We can stand for the mine to be shut down longer than they can stand to wait for us to agree to something we can't afford."

"You seem to have an answer for everything, Jessie," Mason said after a thoughtful pause. "You make a very convincing case. I agree with your reasoning, except for one thing."

"And what is that?"

"I haven't been completely idle, you know. And even if you don't agree with me fully, I think you'll admit that I know a fair amount about copper mining."

"Jared, I don't expect to agree with you about everything, or that you'll agree completely with me. And I'm not underestimating your ability. Now, what is this one thing bothering you that you haven't told me about yet?"

"When I began to get reports that our production was falling off, I decided to do some prospecting. That's how I started out, you remember."

"Yes, of course I remember. What did you find?"

"Nothing. Absolutely no traces of copper anywhere within the ten-mile circle I covered beyond the end of our longest tunnel. As I said, Jessie, there's a real possibility that we're working the last of the lode."

"I must say that doesn't sound encouraging."

"No. My prospecting samples and the tests are at the assay office in Copperopolis. I left them there until all the samples were assayed, and haven't picked them up yet. I think you ought to see them, Jessie."

"Of course I should," Jessie agreed.

"Then why don't I go back to town and get them? The sooner you look at them, the better."

"That's a good idea, Jared. I want to see them, of course. But before you leave, there are a few questions I'd like to ask you about the figures on some of those last statements. It won't take long, and then, when I've seen the assay figures, I'll have a better basis for deciding the best thing to do."

Chapter 10

Ki rode into Copperopolis just after sunset and left the horse at the livery stable. Staying away from the main street, he circled around to Belle's house. There was a light shining through the bedroom window, and the shade was up. He tapped at the door and Belle let him in.

"He hasn't gotten here yet, Ki," she said. "But hurry anyhow."

"I will." Ki was already heading for the trapdoor. He put the chair beneath it and pushed it up, then said, "I hope you've got a spare blanket I can use, Belle. Those rafters are going to get pretty hard if I have to stay up here long."

Belle went into the bedroom and came back with a blanket. Ki levered himself up through the opening and she returned the chair to the kitchen. Looking down at her, Ki cautioned, "Now don't act worried in front of Mason and Goodwin. Just forget about me being up here."

"All right, Ki. I'll try."

Replacing the trapdoor, Ki waited until his eyes adjusted to the gloom, then crawled across the ceiling joists until he judged that he was over the living room. Arranging the blanket to cover the edges of the boards, he stretched out and waited.

Goodwin was the first to arrive. Ki heard a light tapping, then Belle's voice.

"Jared's not here yet, Mr. Goodwin. But he shouldn't be too long. Come in and sit down."

"Thanks, Belle." There was a sharp click of a door clos-

106

ing, then Goodwin said, "You know, Belle, Mason's a lucky man to have a nice girl like you looking after him."

"Well, thank you, Mr. Goodwin. Would you like a drink while you're waiting for Jared?"

"Don't mind if I do."

Ki found that the ceiling just beneath his ears acted as a resonator, and transmitted every sound from the room below. Not only were voices clearly audible, but he could reconstruct what was going on from the noises that reached his keen ears. Goodwin's heavy tread thunked across the floor, and there was a creaking of springs as he sat down in one of the armchairs. Belle's lighter, quicker footsteps and the clink of glass on glass told him when she poured Goodwin's drink and carried it to him.

"I'm sure Jared won't keep you waiting long," she said.

"Since I've got such good company, I don't mind a bit. Why don't you pour a drink for yourself, Belle? I don't want to be a solitary drinker."

"Well—I guess just a little one."

"I'd imagine you get lonesome here, all by yourself all day, while Jared's out at the mine," Goodwin suggested.

"Oh, I keep busy. I've got—" Belle stopped as the rasp of a key turning a lock reached Ki's ears. She went on, "Here's Jared now."

Mason's heavy voice followed the noise of the door closing.

"Sorry I kept you waiting, Saul. Belle, pour me a drink and set the bottle over here where we can reach it. Then you can go do something in the other room while Saul and I talk." After the noises of movement had died away, the mine superintendent went on, "I had to stay at the mine longer than I intended to. Jessie Starbuck's here."

"So I heard," Goodwin said.

"Damned if you don't know more about what goes on

at the mine than I do, Saul! I wish I had your bunch of spies."

"Not spies, Jared," Goodwin said, then added, "Concerned brothers in the Knights of Labor."

"Brothers, shit! You'd throw them over in a minute, if it suited you."

"Jared, you shock me," Goodwin said self-righteously. "You know I'd never betray my loyal brothers!" But then he chuckled and added, "At least not as long as they serve my purposes, and bring me a comfortable living with their monthly dues."

"I think I'm in the wrong business," Mason said. There was a clink of glassware, then his voice became serious as he went on, "I don't think Jessie Starbuck's going to fit into our plan. She didn't warm up a bit when I hinted that she ought to think about selling the mines."

"She needs convincing reasons, you should know that. How long do you think it will take you to change her mind?"

"After talking to her, I'm not sure I *can* change her mind, Saul. She's like her father, stubborn as a goddamned mule."

In his attic hideaway, Ki smiled. He knew even better than Jared Mason just how determined Jessie could be.

"Time isn't on our side, either," Goodwin said thoughtfully. "The buyers I've told you about won't keep their money tied up forever."

"If they want the Starbuck mines, they'll just have to hold on until I can work on Jessie and bring her around." Glass tinkled on glass again and Mason added, "Hold your glass over, Saul, so I can refill it."

Goodwin said, "This isn't the only proposition they're interested in, Jared. And don't forget, if the deal I've made with them falls through, I might not find another group that will cut you in for a share in the new company unless you've got cash to match theirs."

"You know I haven't got that kind of money!"

"Then put the pressure on the Starbuck woman, Jared."

"It's not my fault she's so pigheaded, damn it! But I think I can bring her around, if I've got a little time."

"How much time?"

"How can I tell? She never stays anywhere long. I might not be able to talk her into selling before she leaves."

"That's not good enough, Jared," Goodwin said. "My people want the Starbuck mine proposition settled so they can move in on the Anaconda while Daly's busy trying to get the state capital moved here to Copperopolis."

"Do they really intend to take on Daly and Hearst?"

"Certainly. It won't be as simple as taking over the Starbuck mines ought to be, if you do your job right. That's why I'm spending so much time organizing the Knights of Labor. Money alone won't buy out Daly and Hearst."

"Money might not buy out Jessie Starbuck, either, Saul. She's got just about as much of it as those two put together."

"Perhaps I've been underestimating your employer," Goodwin said thoughtfully. "Some extra pressure might move her faster than figures on a sheet of paper."

"What kind of pressure?"

"My enforcers, of course. My Knights of Labor."

"Hell, they're just miners figuring to organize into a union so they can squeeze higher pay out of us!"

"That's what the public and the mine operators see. I thought you understood me better by now, Jared."

His voice puzzled, Mason said, "I guess I still don't."

"Violent action does not arouse public sympathy unless the violence can be seen as advancing a good cause. And what could be a better cause than a poor working man forced to fight a heartless employer to get a fair wage?"

"I'm beginning to see now," Mason said. "No wonder you're so certain you can take over the Anaconda after you get the Starbuck mines! If Daly doesn't give in, you close him down!"

"And there are many ways of doing that, my friend," Goodwin went on. "My enforcers are not nice men. They learned their lessons from some of the old Molly Maguires, but I've taught them not to make the mistakes the Mollies made."

"They still torture people, don't they?"

"Certainly not! Their enemies are not other miners, but the mine operators. Torture is out of style. They use a charge of blasting powder in one of the stopes, a fight among the miners that will stop production for several days, a fire in the office, an ore train wrecked on its way from the mine to the smelter—I have a wide choice of weapons, Jared." There was a short silence, then Goodwin said, "No. No more for me."

His voice a bit thicker than it had been, Mason said, "How many enforcers do you have, for God's sake? You've got to have a lot more than I figured, if you can do all that."

"Don't ask me for confidential information, Jared," Goodwin replied, his voice suddenly cold. "I have enough to do all the things I've mentioned."

"Twenty?" Mason asked.

"Ten, twenty, thirty—make your own guess. As I told you, I have enough."

Ki heard the same squeaking of chair springs he'd heard before, when Goodwin sat down. This time he surmised that Goodwin was standing up. He stretched carefully to relieve his muscles, which were stiff from lack of motion.

"You're not leaving, Saul!" Mason protested. "We've still got a few things to talk about."

"No. You're mistaken, Jared. You have a few things to think about, and I'll leave you to do just that. Get word to me in the usual way when you have something positive to tell me. And don't bother to see me to the door."

Ki heard no movement in the room below after the back

door closed with a sharp bang behind Goodwin. He strained his ears, but all he heard were undefinable sounds of movement. Then Belle's voice came through the ceiling.

"Jared! Why do you have to drink out of the bottle, like a heathen? There's a glass on the table right beside you."

"Oh, shut up, Belle," Mason growled. "I don't need you to teach me manners."

"I'm sorry, Jared. I didn't mean to scold you," Belle said. "Did something happen between you and Mr. Goodwin that's upset you? He slammed the door when he left."

"Nothing's wrong. Come on, let's get to bed. I've got to be back at the mine early tomorrow, and I didn't have time to stay with you this morning. Maybe you can make me feel better."

"Sure I can. I always do, don't I?" Belle's voice was low and soothing. Then she said, "But I ought to straighten up in here, and I think you need to walk around in the fresh air for a minute or two."

"I don't need anything but you, right now," Mason replied. "Stop arguing and let's go."

Ki had been getting ready to move quickly, but he settled down again. He hoped that Mason would go to sleep quickly; his body was becoming painfully cramped after his long session of being draped across the narrow edges of the rafters with only a folded blanket for a cushion.

To ease the strain, he took advantage of the movements of Belle and Mason and the noises they were making as they moved to the bedroom. On all fours, Ki crawled across the rafters until he reached the trapdoor. Spreading the blanket as best he could in the darkness, he settled down again for what he hoped would be a short wait.

He had not realized how close he was to the bedroom until he heard the first sounds coming through the ceiling. The footsteps of one of them, he could not tell which one, moved from the kitchen to the bedroom. The door clicked as it closed. He heard the rustling of their clothing as they undressed, and when they began talking, their voices reached him almost as plainly as they had in the living room.

"I'm sorry you didn't have a better talk with Mr. Goodwin," Belle said. "It's got you all upset, I can see that."

"Oh, that wasn't anything that matters, Belle. We just had different ideas about something, that's all."

"But it'll be all right, whatever you and he are working on?" she asked anxiously.

"Sure it will. I've got Goodwin right where I want him."

"I guess I don't understand," Belle said, her voice showing that she was puzzled but trying to please.

"Well, there's things women don't see the way men do, Belle. Now, I saw Marcus Daly strutting around down in Virginia City while I was there. He acts like he owns the damn place!"

"From the way everybody talks, he almost does."

"That won't last forever!" Mason's tone was boastfully gloating. "Goodwin's got him on his list to knock off, and he's figuring on putting me in Daly's place. But what Goodwin doesn't know is that I'm smarter than he thinks I am. Once I'm set, I'll get rid of him, and then we'll see who does the strutting."

"Well, if that's what you want, I'm glad. But what's going to become of me when you get to be such a big man?"

"You'll move right up with me, Belle, wherever I go." Mason said, his voice a bit slurred now. "You don't think I could do without what you've got, do you? Damn! I get hot just looking at you standing there bare-ass naked!"

Ki heard a new sound, which took him a few minutes to identify as bare feet padding across the floor. Then Belle broke the silence with a giggle.

"Now stop that, Jared. You know how ticklish I am there!"

"I love the way you jiggle when I rub you, Belle!"

"If you want to know the truth, I sort of like it."

"I know what you like better, though," Mason said. "Come on, let's get to bed."

There was a rustle of bedclothes, followed by a prolonged silence. Then another few minutes of small, unidentifiable sounds reached Ki's ears. After that there was a long silence, finally broken by Belle's voice.

"It's all right, Jared," she said soothingly. "You know it takes you a while, sometimes. Just wait a minute."

"I don't feel like waiting, damn it!" Mason told her. "Lay back and let me kiss your titties, Belle. That usually does the trick."

Another prolonged silence followed. Ki could picture the scene below him. He did not relish the role in which he'd been inadvertently cast, but he had no choice. No amount of willpower could keep him from hearing the voices below.

Mason said, "That's not doing anything for me!"

"It will, Jared," Belle replied. "Here. I'll just take hold of you and help a little bit."

After several minutes, Mason said, "That's not doing a thing for me, Belle. Go on, take your hand away and get your head down there."

"Jared, I—"

"Shut up and do it, damn it!" Mason snarled.

When Mason began a soft moaning, Ki pictured the scene below and decided that even if he made a small noise, neither of the bedroom's occupants would be aware of it. Taking his slippers off, he tucked them in the waistband of his trousers. Silently he lifted the trapdoor and eased himself through it.

Then, hanging by his hands from the rim of the opening,

he dropped the few feet to the floor. When his bare feet touched the floor they made only a whisper of noise, and it was blanketed by Mason's animal growls of satisfaction. Ki padded out the back door and was swallowed by the night.

★

Chapter 11

Copperopolis was far from asleep when Ki hurried down its main street. The stores and cafes were closed, but the saloons were still lighted and, though not overcrowded, were reasonably well patronized. The town, Ki thought as he walked briskly toward the livery stable, was a small-scale version of Nevada's Virginia City, where miners also worked on shifts, and the lights in the bars were never turned off. He reached the livery stable and roused the night attendant, who made quick work of saddling the rented horse. In less than a half hour after leaving Belle's, Ki was on his way through the darkness on the rutted road that led to Starhope and the mines.

Starhope's houses were dark when he passed the little town. The night-shift miners had left for their jobs, and those coming home from the preceding shift had already gone to bed. Beyond the town, however, lights still glowed through the windows of the mine office.

Ki reined in and went up the steps to the narrow porch that ran along the front of the building. Through the window beside the door he saw Jessie, still at work on the paper-strewn desk at the rear of the office. He knocked. Jessie looked up, frowned, and came to open the door.

"Oh, it's you, Ki," she said when she saw who was standing in the light streaming through the doorway. "Why didn't you just come on in? The door isn't locked."

"It should be," Ki replied. "At this time of night, and

you here alone. The window shades should be drawn, too."

"Why? I'm perfectly safe here."

"Perhaps not as safe as you think, Jessie."

Jessie pulled aside the jacket she was wearing to show Ki her holstered Colt. She said, "Even if I don't expect trouble, I try to be ready for it."

"Your pistol wouldn't be much protection from a sharp-shooter with a rifle, hidden by the darkness."

"From the way you're talking, Ki, I gather you've found out something in town?"

"Quite a number of things."

"Come on in, then. This is as good a place to talk as any, at this time of night. We can draw the shades if you're worried."

"Perhaps it would be better if we went upstairs. Have you had supper, by the way?"

"Of course." Jessie sounded surprised. "Haven't you?"

"Not yet. I've been too busy."

"We'll go upstairs, then. I'll leave the lights on down here. Jared is supposed to be back from town with some reports from the assay office."

"I doubt that you'll see Jared Mason before morning, Jessie. When I left town he was having a struggle with what seem to be two of his chief preoccupations, liquor and lust."

Jessie smiled and said, "Well, if Jared's not coming back, there's no point in my staying down here. Let's put out the lights and lock up, then we'll go upstairs and you can tell me what you've found out."

In the kitchen of the upstairs apartment, Ki found a small bed of coals in the cookstove. He fed them a bit of kindling and soon had a cooking fire going. He put on a skillet and, while waiting for it to heat, said to Jessie, "I'm glad I got here before Mason, even if I don't look for him to show up before morning."

116

"Do you want to talk now, or wait until you've eaten?" Jessie asked.

"It doesn't matter. I'm just going to cook some ham and eggs; they're the easiest and quickest food we've got on hand."

"Tell me what happened, then. From the little you've said, you've found out a lot of things we should have known before."

"More things than I like," Ki told her, putting a slice of ham in the skillet. "I'm surprised you waited for Mason all this time, but from what I turned up in Copperopolis, I don't think he had any intention of coming back here tonight."

"I lost track of time, working on those reports," Jessie said. "I came up here and fixed a bite of supper right after the men in the office went home. Then I remembered that Jared was supposed to bring me some assay reports, so I went downstairs to wait for him, and started trying to reconcile those statements again while I waited. You seem to know what happened to Jared to keep him from coming back."

Ki looked around from the stove, where he was breaking eggs into the skillet with the ham. He said, "Three things happened to him, Jessie. Saul Goodwin, too much whiskey, and the woman he's keeping in town."

Jessie ignored everything but the most important part of Ki's disclosure. Going directly to the point, she asked, "Goodwin? The Knights of Labor man?"

"Yes. But the Knights of Labor should really be called the Knights of Goodwin. They're his version of the Molly Maguires, his enforcers."

"But what about the Knights of Labor, Ki? They were a real union when they started."

"If there's anything left of the Knights of Labor, it's not in Montana, Jessie. Goodwin admitted that to Mason tonight. Goodwin himself *is* the Knights of Labor in Copperopolis, and I suppose in Virginia City too. He plans to organize the men here first, and then move on to the Anaconda."

"What did Mason have to say to that?"

"Nothing that he should have, considering the job he holds. He's sold out to Goodwin."

Rapidly, Ki sketched for Jessie the conversation he'd overheard between the two men. He stopped at the point where Goodwin had left Belle's house. When he'd finished, Jessie sat in thoughtful silence for several moments.

"I see now that I've made a serious mistake, Ki," she said at last. "Trusting Mason as far as I did, leaving him to run the mines without supervising him closely."

"You only did what was natural, Jessie. Until now, Mason's been a good man."

"Yes," Jessie agreed. "And Alex trusted him completely."

"Men go wrong, even the best of them," Ki said matter-of-factly. "And when they do, most of the time nobody can really say why. But I think the reason Mason did is pretty clear."

"A minute ago you said something about whiskey and lust," Jessie reminded Ki. "But when you were telling me what Goodwin and Jared talked about, you didn't mention the connection."

"Oh, while he was talking with Goodwin, Mason was drinking pretty constantly. I'm not excusing him, but some of the things Goodwin said threw him pretty badly off balance."

"Jared was never a heavy drinker," Jessie frowned. "But I suppose that's another of the ways he's changed."

"You'd know his past record better than I would. You came here a time or two with Alex, and I wasn't always

118

along. That was when I was just the foreman at the Circle Star."

"You were never 'just the foreman' of the ranch, Ki. Alex valued your views about other things, just as I do." Jessie stood up and went to the range, where she put the kettle on. "I need a cup of tea. I have a feeling there's still quite a bit of your story still to come."

Ki did not reply for a moment. He was mentally editing the rest of the disclosures he'd be making of his night's discoveries, and made time to think while he slid the ham and eggs from the skillet onto a plate.

"Yes. Quite a bit," he agreed. "But let me start eating before my supper gets cold, Jessie. I've already told you the most important part."

"Go ahead, Ki. I need to do some thinking while I drink my tea, anyhow."

After the dangers they'd shared and overcome, there was no need for words between them. He ate in silence and she sipped her tea. Ki finished and pushed away his plate before he began answering Jessie's unasked questions.

"You haven't asked me, and I haven't had time to tell you, what kept me in Copperopolis so late when I had my brush with Boston last night," he began. "But when—"

"Ki," Jessie broke in. "You don't have to explain anything to me. We've always had our own private lives, without any need to talk about them."

"This time, talking about mine is necessary," Ki said. "I told you that Boston was annoying a young lady in the store. She offered to attend to the cut on my cheek, and I went home with her. It wasn't until Mason showed up unexpectedly that I found out she was his mistress."

"I see," Jessie said noncommittally, when Ki stopped. "And having discovered that, you almost certainly stumbled

119

on the link we didn't know about between Jared and Saul Goodwin."

"Yes," Ki replied. "I found that out by accident, too."

Jessie went on quickly, her voice still calmly neutral, "So, somewhere and somehow, you also learned that Jared was to meet Goodwin at the lady's house, went back to town, and managed to persuade her to arrange for you to overhear the conversation you've just told me about between Jared and Saul Goodwin."

"That sums it up very well, Jessie," Ki replied. His voice and face were as expressionless as hers. "It just happened that after Goodwin left, I couldn't get out of the place where she'd hidden me. Mason was quite drunk by then, and though it wasn't my choice to stay, I was forced to. So I happened to overhear some pillow-talk between him and Belle."

"Belle being the young lady, of course," Jessie said, her voice still flat and without inflection.

"Of course. From what I heard, I could deduce that Mason has been drinking heavily for quite some time, and that he's become driven by the ambition to take Marcus Daly's place as the leading citizen of Montana."

For a moment, Jessie stared at Ki without speaking. Then she asked, "Is Jared serious about that, Ki?"

"Oh yes. Very much so."

Sighing, Jessie shook her head. "Now I can understand a lot of things that didn't make sense, Ki. Once an idea like that takes hold of a man's mind, he loses a lot of things. They include good judgment, honesty, and loyalty. And Jared's mistress is young and attractive, I'm sure."

"Much younger than he is, but older than you or me," Ki said. "And, as you say, attractive."

Jessie frowned and said thoughtfully, "Jared's wife died a few years after he came to work for Alex. He's been a widower for quite a long time. An attractive woman wouldn't have much trouble manipulating him."

"I don't think that's what's happening in this case, Jessie. Belle's not an ambitious woman. If there's any manipulation, it's being done by Goodwin. But my hunch is that Jared's just gotten ambitious, and Goodwin's taking advantage of it."

Still frowning, Jessie sat silently for several minutes. As her silence continued, Ki got up and poured himself a cup of tea from the pot she had brewed. Then he went back to the table, sat down, and waited for Jessie to speak.

"I just remembered something you said earlier, Ki, and it's given me an idea. You heard Goodwin say that he plans to organize the men here in the Starbuck mines and then move on to the Anaconda. That would give him virtual control of most of the copper output of Montana."

"Yes, of course it would. He could close down the mines if he had enough Knights of Labor to follow his orders."

"Montana produces most of the copper mined in the United States, Ki. If the Knights of Labor succeed here, wouldn't it be easy to extend their influence all over the country?"

"I'd think so."

"Ki." Jessie's voice was very sober. "Who's interested in monopolies?"

There was silence for a moment as they simply looked at each other. Then Ki nodded and said softly, "The cartel."

"Yes," Jessie replied. "Interesting, isn't it? Once you've dealt with them enough, you can almost *feel* it when you come across something they're involved in. Somehow they're connected with Goodwin and the Knights of Labor." She paused and sipped her tea, then went on, "The cartel would start with the Starbuck mines, of course. If they did succeed in getting control of these mines, it would give them a foothold to use in taking over the Anaconda. After that, it would be easy to take over the country's entire copper industry, one mine or smelter at a time."

"And from there it would be easy to move into other metals, and with that much of a grip—"

"We both know what would happen, Ki," Jessie broke in.

"Yes. But I can't see anything we can do tonight," Ki said. "And I need sleep now as much as I needed food a few minutes ago. Can't we put off any more talk until breakfast?"

"That's what I was about to suggest. We came out here just to clear up a problem at the mine, but we're facing a bigger job now. We'll sleep on it, and start fresh in the morning."

"I know it's impossible to watch two men at once," Jessie told Ki as they stood outside the office the next morning. The sun had not yet risen, but dawn had driven darkness from the sky. She went on, "I have an idea that Jared will hurry out here as soon as he sobers up. I'll handle him when he gets here. Your job is to keep track of Goodwin."

"If you need me, send young Johanssen to town after me. In a town as small as Copperopolis, I shouldn't be hard to find."

"There shouldn't be any trouble here, Ki. I'm going to do something that I wouldn't ordinarily. I intend to search Mason's office. If we can find something connecting him with Goodwin, it might be helpful in getting him to talk."

With a wave, Ki rode off down the rutted road. Jessie unlocked the office door and went inside. At that hour, the men had not yet shown up for work. She went first to the desk where she'd been working the night before, and began gathering up the papers that were spread over its top. She

122

was still sorting and arranging them when McKelway came in.

"Good morning, Mr. McKelway," Jessie greeted him.

"Morning, Jessie," McKelway replied, hanging his coat and hat on one of the hooks behind the door. "It don't look to me like you've moved since yesterday when I left. Don't tell me you've been here all night."

"Oh no. I just came in. Do you always get here at this time of the morning? The office doesn't open until seven-thirty."

"Old men like me don't need much sleep, Jessie. But I'm generally the first one here. I like to get an early start."

McKelway opened one of the drawers of his desk and took out a pair of black cambric sleeve protectors, which he pulled over the cuffs and lower arms of his snow-white shirt. He settled a green visor on his head, sat down at his desk, and began taking ledgers off the shelf behind him.

One of the heavy leatherbound tomes slipped from his hands and fell to the floor. Several sheets of paper dropped from the book as it was falling, and one of them floated across the narrow gap between his desk and the one Jessie was using. She picked up the sheet and had started to hand it to the old man when the writing on it caught her eyes. She withdrew the paper and held it where she could see it more clearly.

"Oh, that's not anything important, Jessie," McKelway said quickly. "Likely just a note I scribbled to myself not to forget something."

"It doesn't seem to me to be a memorandum to yourself," she replied quietly. "It looks as though you started to write a letter to me and didn't finish it."

McKelway looked over the top of his spectacles at the sheet of paper and started toward Jessie's desk. He said, "Maybe you better let me look at that."

Jessie spread the paper out on the desktop, but held it firmly with her hand. McKelway tried to pick it up, but she gently pushed his hand away.

"Unless you know somebody else named Jessie, it's addressed to me," she said, reading from the sheet. "'Dear Jessie: It's been a long time since you've been here to the mines. Even if it isn't any of my affair, I think you ought to know—'" She raised her head and caught McKelway's eyes, held them with her own, and asked quietly, "What is it that I ought to know?"

"Now I just can't recall right this minute, Jessie," the old man stammered. "Maybe some little thing that was in my mind at one time or the other. I don't rightly remember—"

"Mr. McKelway," Jessie broke in quietly, "I have a letter here in my pocket that I'd like you to look at."

With her free hand, Jessie took out the letter addressed to Alex that had first started her interest in the affairs of the mines. She slid it from the envelope and spread it out beside the page she was holding on the desk.

"You know, Mr. McKelway, the writing on these two pages looks remarkably alike to me. Doesn't it to you too?"

"I don't—" McKelway began, then stopped and shook his head. He sighed deeply and went on, "I never was much good at lying, Jessie. You've caught up with me, so I'm not going to beat around the bush any longer."

"You did write this letter addressed to Alex, then?"

"Yes."

"As long as you're telling me things, I've got another question to ask you," Jessie continued. "The second night Ki and I got to Copperopolis, before we came out to the mine, we were staying at the Miner's Rest. Did you come to my room that night and warn me about being in danger?"

McKelway's answer came without hesitation this time.

124

"Yes, Jessie. That was me too."

"Don't you think you'd better explain what all this beating around the bush means?" she asked.

"Well," the old man said, "I suppose the first thing I need to do is apologize to you."

"You don't need to apologize at all," Jessie replied. "But surely you've known me long enough to know that if you had something important to tell me about the mines, I'd listen to you."

"Deep down, I guess I did, but—well, old men get to be a little bit afraid of things without any cause, I guess. I know I did when I pulled those two childish tricks."

"Why did you feel you had to address this letter to Alex instead of me?" Jessie asked.

"You can see from that first letter I started that I wanted to, Jessie," McKelway said. "Then I just got to thinking that you must get a lot of mail from fools, and you might not remember me or pay any attention to a letter like the one I began writing."

"So you wrote a letter to Alex, thinking it would get my attention better than one addressed to me?"

"That's about the size of it," McKelway sighed. "I ought to've known you hadn't changed, but it'd been a long time since you'd been here, and I felt like I couldn't be sure."

"But why did you try to make me believe the letter was written by some woman who lives in Starhope?"

"There's only three of us working in the office here, Jessie. If I'd written you without signing my name, you'd have known it had to be me or Fred or Eric. I didn't want you to write to Jared Mason asking him to find out who'd written it. That could have cost all of us our jobs."

"And the stunt at the hotel? When you played ghost, or whatever it was you expected me to take you for?"

"Let me ask you a question, Jessie," McKelway said.

125

"If a clerk in an office complains about his boss to the owner of the place, what's the first thing the owner's likely to think?"

"Normally, I suppose it would be that the clerk's trying to get his boss into trouble."

"That's just what I thought," McKelway said. "So that's why I rigged that fool get-up when I passed a closet in the hall where I knew the hotel kept extra bedding."

"Well, I'm certainly glad to get those mysteries explained," Jessie sighed. "But now that I know you've got something important on your mind, don't you think it's about time to tell me what it is?"

Chapter 12

"It's far past time for me to tell you, Jessie," McKelway replied. "You can't imagine how guilty I've felt."

"Guilty?" Jessie asked. "About what?"

"Not having the courage to write you when I first suspected Jared Mason of sending you false information."

"How long has he been doing it?" Jessie asked.

Before McKelway could answer, Fred Edmonds came into the office. After they'd exchanged greetings, he said, "You early birds make me feel a little uncomfortable, even if I am on time."

"There's no need for you to," Jessie told him. "Because Mr. McKelway and I are going to make up for that extra time by playing hookey for a little while. I've been here two days, and I haven't even looked at the mines yet."

"Are you planning to go into the drifts?" Edmonds asked.

"Oh no. Not today, though I do want to do that before I leave. We won't be gone very long." She turned to McKelway and said, "Come on, we'll talk as we take that little walk."

When they got outside the office and began walking along the bumpy, rutted road that led to the mine shafts, McKelway said, "Thank you for not scolding me, Jessie. Or maybe you're saving that for later."

"I haven't any intention of scolding you," Jessie assured him. "You took what you thought was the best way to warn me."

"But I should have done it earlier, when Jared first began acting strange. He didn't change suddenly; it was so gradual that I didn't notice it at first. Then when I looked back, I realized that he hadn't been behaving the way he used to for quite a while."

"And you didn't know why?"

McKelway shook his head. "No. I'm still not sure I do, but I guess stealing from the company would make him change."

"Jared's been with us long enough to know that if he needed money, I'd be glad to lend it to him," Jessie said. "When did you first start getting suspicious?"

"Well, like I said, it didn't come to me all at once."

"Say, six months ago?"

"About then. That was when Jared began mailing the monthly reports and the quarterly statements himself, instead of giving them to me to mail."

"How did that happen, Mr. McKelway? Did he start by just mailing an occasional report, or did he do it suddenly?"

"Very suddenly. I gave him a monthly report to sign, and he put it on his desk and told me he'd sign it later. The next day I asked him for the report to mail, and he said he'd mailed it himself."

"And after that he mailed all the reports himself?"

"Yes. The third or fourth month, I offered to put the report in with the regular mail. I recall that it was a stormy day, and Eric had to start to town early. Jared said he hadn't had time to check it, and that he'd mail it himself. I suppose I ought to've finished that first letter I started to write you and sent it on, but, well, I just didn't."

"After your explanation, I can understand why. But when you came to my room in the Miner's Rest, you talked about danger. Losing money isn't very pleasant, but it's not dangerous."

"It could be for the mines, Jessie, and for the people who live at Starhope. But when I said what I did about danger, I wasn't just thinking about money. I remember back when the Knights of Labor were sending their Molly Maguires around to torture and maim people that were against them. When I found out you were here, I got worried about them hurting you."

McKelway's association of the Knights of Labor with the danger they might present to her rang a bell in Jessie's mind. She asked him, "The changes you noticed in Jared started right after you heard about the Knights of Labor trying to organize the miners, didn't it?"

After he'd thought for a moment, McKelway said, "A little while after we first heard about the Knights of Labor."

They walked on in silence for a few minutes. Thanks to Ki's discoveries, the reason for Jared Mason's actions did not puzzle Jessie as they did McKelway. She could see the connection between Mason's actions and Saul Goodwin's sudden appearance in Copperopolis, though concrete evidence of their collusion was still lacking. Before she confronted Mason with his misdeeds, Jessie wanted a great deal more information than she now had.

Their walk had brought them to the entrance of the broad, round, bowl-like valley where the mine tunnels began. The dirt road and the tracks of the railroad spur came together here to pass through the gap leading to the valley. The ties of the railroad line offered easier walking than the road, and talking became too difficult as McKelway led the way along the ties and through the wide opening.

In the valley, the railroad spur branched off into a maze of sidings that covered the valley floor. The three main sidings led to the shaft heads of the three mines. Amid the tracks were scattered a number of small, rough buildings, little more than sheds. On several of the sidings were strings of ore gondolas; on some sidings the cars were full, and on others they were empty. Every other day a locomotive arrived, pulling a train of empty gondolas. These would be placed on a siding, and the loaded cars from other sidings would be coupled onto the locomotive to be hauled out of the valley and off to the Anaconda smelter. From each mine entrance emerged a wooden trestle onto which could be pulled the smaller ore carts that ran along the drifts. The larger gondolas were brought up underneath the trestle, where the contents of the ore carts could be dumped into them.

Except for the few men at work moving cars, and the tracks and shacks, there was surprisingly little evidence that the mines were being worked. As she gazed across the wide floor of the valley, Jessie remembered vividly the few occasions when she'd entered the mines themselves.

She'd learned during her visits underground that the stopes were worked only until they reached the end of the copper lode. Eventually the amount of copper in the earth no longer justified the labor required to dig several pounds of dirt in order to extract the few ounces of copper and the even smaller quantity of silver it contained. When a stope was worked out, its entrance was boarded up and the main tunnel extended to the point where a new stope was opened.

There were three main shafts leading into the depths, where the raw ore was dug by men wielding picks and shovels. Jessie had never forgotten what she'd seen on her visits underground. Calcium lanterns spaced widely apart below tiny airshafts lighted the main drift, its roof and sides shored up with heavy timbers and sturdy boards, where the ore carts were lined up in front of the stopes. Except for its small size, the tunnel was little different from those used by railroad trains.

She'd gone into some of the stopes, passing through small shafts that led to the working faces. There was little or no shoring in these shafts, which were barely wide enough to allow the passage of the ore carts, and led into huge underground chambers. There were no lights in the stopes or chambers except those provided by the little calcium-burning helmet lanterns the miners wore. The men who worked in them talked little, so the depths of the stopes were silent except for the soft thudding of picks and the guttural scraping of shovels as the miners dug their picks deep into the walls and pried out huge clods of earth, which they shoveled into the carts.

Looking at the openings of the three main shafts, Jessie could easily recreate the scenes beyond their yawning mouths. She had no desire to go into them again, for she had not found the surroundings appealing. She remembered the semi-darkness, the miners appearing suddenly like ghosts in the gloom, and most of all the air that was breathable, but laden with an amalgam of odors. There was the undefinable scent given off by the raw soil, the harsh, biting tang of the fumes from calcium lamps and lanterns, and the sour aroma of sweat from crusted dungarees and jackets that had been worn too long.

"It hasn't changed a bit since I first saw it," Jessie said to McKelway as they stood looking over the valley.

"All the changes are underground," McKelway told her. "The shafts are a bit longer and there are more old stopes closed, but you'd not be likely to notice that."

"Jared told me that the mines aren't producing as much ore as they used to," she said.

"Oh, it always varies, Jessie. Some stopes will seem to be petering out, then the faces will go into a new stratum and start producing well again."

"As soon as Ki and I have worked out our problems, I'll have to go underground and see what it's like now," she said thoughtfully. "But right now I think I'd better get back to the office and pick up where I left off."

They started back along the tracks, walking single-file as before. After they'd reached the mouth of the valley and could walk abreast again, Jessie turned to McKelway and asked, "Does Jared keep a file of reports in his office?"

"Oh, to be sure, he does. It saves him a lot of time when he's looking for something, even if what he wants is out in the office, in the big files."

"I think I'd better have a look at Jared's private files," Jessie said thoughtfully.

"That's easy to do. Fred's got a key to his office."

They reached the office. Eric Johanssen had arrived during their absence and was working at his desk, beside the one Jessie had been using. Jessie went to Edmonds's desk.

"I want to cross-check some of the figures in the statements I've been working on with those Jared keeps in his office," she said. "Would you give me the key to it, please?"

Edmonds hesitated for a moment, then opened one of the drawers of his desk. Pulling it out full length, he took out a key that had been hanging from a hook on the back. As he handed the key to Jessie, he said, "Mr. Mason instructed me not to open his office except in an emergency, Miss Starbuck, but since everything around here is your property, I'm sure he won't mind me giving it to you."

"Thank you. I'm going to work in Jared's office for a while, and I'll depend on you to see that I'm not disturbed."

After gathering up the statements from the desk she'd been using, Jessie unlocked Mason's private office and went in. She closed the door behind her and looked around. The office was unchanged since her last visit. Mason's desk was an imposing oak rolltop model that stood against the rear wall of the room. It had a shallow center drawer and three drawers on one side of the knee-hole and two on the other, one of them being a double-depth drawer designed to hold files.

132

A wide oak table stood in front of the desk; a tall lamp with a green dome-shaped shade was on the table, and a swivel chair between it and the desk. A pair of oak file cases occupied one corner of the room. Except for a small potbellied stove against the outer wall, the only other furniture in the office was a cellarette cased in oak, and a tall hat rack that stood just inside the door.

Depositing her papers on the table, Jessie pulled on the handle of the desktop. It did not budge. She looked at the drawers. They had no keyholes in them, but when she tried to open each of them in turn, she found that they too were locked. They were, she thought, like the drawers of Alex's desk—when the rolltop was locked, the bolt pressed on a plunger that automatically locked the drawers.

For a moment, Jessie looked at the desk, then she took from her purse the key to her father's rolltop desk. She tried the key in the lock; it resisted at first, but when she worked the bit from side to side and exerted a little force on the key, the lock yielded reluctantly. She rolled up the top and tried the drawers. They opened easily now. Sitting down, Jessie opened the file drawer.

Working methodically from front to back, she lifted out each folder and examined its contents, fanning through the sheets with agile fingers. None of the files contained anything except the sort of routine correspondence that might be found in any office: letters and orders from the metal-fabricating firms that bought copper from the mine; communications from the distributors who handled the bulk sale of ingots to smaller manufacturers; copies of letters from Mason answering inquiries about purchasing copper.

Jessie wasted little time on these. After glancing at each of the files to be sure they contained nothing in which she might be interested, she ran her fingers along the underside of the crosspiece between the top and bottom drawers. She found the recessed button she was sure would be there, and pressed it while pulling the drawer out farther. The drawer slid out several inches, revealing a narrow compartment behind the false rear partition. The compartment was crammed with manila envelopes.

Lifting out the envelopes, she spread them on the table. In Mason's handwriting, each of the dozen or so envelopes bore a word or two describing its contents. Jessie pushed aside those that were labeled "report" or "statement," and bore dates going as far back as seven months. She was sure that some would contain reports showing the correct figures of ore production, assay runs showing the amount of copper and silver in the ore from each stope, while others would show the mines' receipts and operating costs.

She was also certain by now that the figures would differ from the files she had brought with her from the outer office and the copies that had been sent to her at the Circle Star.

Three of the big rectangular envelopes remained when Jessie finished putting aside those she would look at later. One of the three was labelled BANK—STARBUCK, another bore the words BANK—PERSONAL. The third bore only one word: GOODWIN. It was the slimmest of the three, and Jessie opened it first.

There were only a few sheets of paper in the envelope. Two of them were letters on stationery imprinted with the heading FARMERS & MECHANICS BANK, 112 SUTTER STREET, SAN FRANCISCO, CALIFORNIA. Jessie remembered that bank well. While in San Francisco sometime earlier, she and Ki had uncovered evidence that it was owned by the cartel.

She scanned the top letter quickly. Addressed to Miss Jessica Starbuck in care of Jared Mason, the letter was only a few lines long. It was an offer to buy the Starbuck copper mines "on behalf of a client of the bank who wishes to remain anonymous for the present, but whose financial situation this bank is prepared to guarantee." The sum offered by the anonymous client was a figure Jessie knew to be far below the mines' real worth.

Jessie looked at the second letter. This one was addressed to Mason and contained two brief paragraphs. The first stipulated that as a condition of the sale, Jared Mason was to be retained as general superintendent at a salary much higher than the one Jessie was paying him. The second paragraph guaranteed that Mason would receive a ten-percent share of the company that would be formed to buy and operate the mines, and would be given a seat on the company's board of directors.

In the envelope marked BANK—STARBUCK, Jessie found a much-corrected draft copy of a letter to the bank in Copperopolis in which the mines' receipts from the sale of copper were deposited. The letter told the bank to follow Mason's verbal instructions in converting checks and bank drafts made out to the Starbuck mines into drafts payable to Mason himself.

Jessie's face was already grim, but when her eyes reached the end of the letter, they glowed angrily. On the half-page of space remaining, her name had been written repeatedly, and with each repetition the forgery of her signature was better. She had no doubt that the final copy of the letter that had gone to the Copperopolis bank had been signed with a forged signature enough like her own to deceive the bank officials.

In the last envelope Jessie found statements from the Virginia City bank covering a period of seven months. The statements were for an account in the name of Jared Mason. Thumbing through the statements, Jessie saw that they reported deposits ranging from $6,000 to $12,000 each month, and the statement bearing the latest date showed that the account now held a total of more than $60,000.

Jessie's face was set in an angry scowl when she finally

leaned back in the oak swivel chair and looked at the documents spread on the table, which proved Jared Mason's treachery beyond any possible doubt. Her fingers drumming on the tabletop, she was considering her next course of action when raised voices coming through the panels of the office door broke into her thoughts.

"I'm very sorry, sir," Fred Edmonds was saying. "Miss Starbuck gave me orders that she was not to be interrupted."

"I don't give a damn who gave you such a stupid order!" came the voice of a second man, and Jessie recognized it as Mason's. "That's my office, and I intend to go in it. Now stand aside!"

There were muted scraping sounds as feet scuffled on the floor outside, then the door was flung open. Jared Mason, his face flushed with anger, stared at Jessie. He stood silent, frozen in place by the shock of seeing the opened desk and drawers, and the papers spread on the table in front of her. Behind him, Edmonds was reeling backward, his arms flailing, as he tried to keep from falling as a result of his scuffle with Mason.

"Come in, Jared," Jessie said before Mason could speak. "You and I have a number of things to discuss."

"Discuss, hell, you nosy little bitch!" Mason snarled. "If you think I'm going to let you rob me of what I've got coming, you're wrong!"

Sweeping his hand inside his coat, Mason drew a revolver. Hampered in her movements by being seated, Jessie reached for her Colt the instant she saw Mason's hand disappear under his jacket.

Behind Mason, Edmonds regained his balance. He saw the gun in Mason's hand and lunged forward, reaching for the weapon.

Hearing Edmonds's footsteps, Mason whirled. Jessie had drawn her Colt by now and was bringing it up.

Mason fired at Edmonds. For a moment Edmonds stood erect, his body arcing backward from the impact of Mason's slug. Then he began crumpling slowly to the floor.

Jessie triggered her Colt as Mason swiveled to bring his pistol around. His second shot hit the tabletop as he began to collapse. The slug plowed across the tough oak, scoring a groove in the wood as it ricocheted and sailed so close to Jessie that she felt the wind of its passing before it thudded into the wall behind her.

Then Mason's revolver dropped from his lifeless hand. The weapon hit the floor with a thud as Mason fell in an ungainly heap and lay still.

Chapter 13

In the front office, McKelway and Eric Johanssen had been frozen at their desks by the sound of Mason's first shot. By the time the answering report rang out from Jessie's Colt, they had recovered from their shock and were on their feet, running toward the door to Mason's office. They watched Mason crumple to the floor, and started again toward the private office, then stopped for the second time beside Fred Edmonds's body. Both men bent over it for a moment, then straightened up.

"He's dead," McKelway said.

Jessie was on her feet now, but had not holstered her Colt. She reached the door connecting the two offices and stopped to glance at Mason's body. Only then did she holster her revolver as she replied to McKelway.

She nodded and said, "So is Jared. I was sure both of them were, from the way they fell. I'm sorry I couldn't get my gun out before he killed poor Fred Edmonds."

"You're all right, aren't you, Jessie?" McKelway asked.

"Of course."

Young Johanssen's face twisted into a puzzled frown as he looked from Jessie to the bodies on the floor. He said, "I don't understand what's going on. What made Mr. Mason so angry that he shot Fred and tried to kill you, Miss Starbuck?"

"I'll explain everything in a minute," Jessie replied as she moved away from Mason's body to go into the large office.

"I think I understand the reason for part of what's happened here," McKelway said. "But things have been going so fast that I'm still a wee bit dizzy."

"Let's sit down," Jessie suggested. She gestured at the bodies. "It's impossible to ignore them, but we'll try, while I explain why things happened the way they did."

With McKelway and Eric hanging on her words, Jessie gave them a quick summary of the letters she'd found hidden in Mason's desk, though she omitted mentioning the cartel. When she'd finished her explanation, McKelway shook his head.

"I'd no idea Jared was stealing from you, Jessie," he said. "But now I understand the reason why he took some of the work Eric and I had been doing away from us and insisted on handling it himself."

Eric nodded. "I guess I can see that much." His youthful face was twisted into a puzzled frown. "Why would Mr. Mason want to turn on you, Miss Jessie, after all the years he'd worked for you and Mr. Starbuck?"

"Envy and ambition, Eric," Jessie replied. "It's ruined many men who were stronger than Jared Mason."

"I hope you've no plans to sell the Starbuck mines, Jessie," McKelway said. "I'd be lost if I didn't have my job here. It's what keeps me feeling young."

"Don't worry," Jessie reassured him. "The mines aren't for sale, and as far as I'm concerned, they won't be. But I'm going to need somebody to fill Jared's job. I hope I can count on you to do that."

"Ah, Jessie, at my age—" McKelway began.

Jessie cut him short. "Forget about age. Take the job and make Eric your assistant. You'll need somebody to do the legwork, though after our walk this morning I think you could handle it quite well." She looked at Eric. "How do you feel about my idea, Eric?"

"I—I don't know what to say, Miss Starbuck. I thought it'd be a long time before I could hope for a job like that."

"You and Mr. McKelway should make a good team," Jessie said encouragingly. "And now that it's settled, let's see what we can do about getting things put in order here. We can sit down and talk about the mines a lot more comfortably after we've finished that unhappy job."

McKelway looked at the two bodies on the floor. "We'll need to bring the sheriff out. And the undertaker."

"I'll ride into town and get them," Eric volunteered.

Jessie said, "I don't want to start by interfering with your decisions, Eric, but suppose you stay here and help Mr. McKelway while I go into Copperopolis. Ki's there, and he needs to know what's happened out here and why. If you'll hitch up the buggy, I'll start right away and get back as soon as I can."

Copperopolis was basking in the noonday sun when Jessie reached its first houses and started up the main street. She had no idea where to look for Ki. He hadn't told her the location of the house where Mason kept Belle, and she couldn't even guess where his investigation of Goodwin and the enforcers might have taken him. Consoling herself with the thought that Copperopolis was a small town with a limited number of places where Ki might be, Jessie guided the buggy slowly along the street, reached its end, turned, and drove through town again, and still she had no idea where else she could begin looking.

She'd noticed the sign of an undertaker on one of the false-front buildings near the depot, and retraced her path through town a third time until she reached it. Going in, she arranged for the undertaker to go to the mine and pick up the bodies of Mason and Edmonds and prepare them for burial. Then she drove the buggy to the sheriff's office to report the two deaths.

On one side of the frame structure that bore the sign DEER LODGE COUNTY COURTHOUSE, a stake topped with an arrow-pointed sign that read SHERIFF pointed to the rear of the building. Jessie found a door and went in. A man wearing a star sat at the desk, and in one corner three men stood talking.

Going to the desk, Jessie said, "I'd like to talk to the sheriff, if he's here."

"You're talking to him, ma'am. Dick Hicks. What can I do for you?"

With no change in the inflection of her voice, she replied, "My name is Jessica Starbuck. I want to report a murder and a killing in self-defense, Sheriff Hicks."

For a moment her words did not sink in. Then Hicks stood up and stared at her for a moment before asking, "You wouldn't have anything to do with the Starbuck mines, would you, ma'am?"

"I own them. The man who committed the murder was Jared Mason, the superintendent. A few hours ago he shot and killed Fred Edmonds, one of the men who works at the mines."

"Jared Mason?" the sheriff asked incredulously.

"Yes."

"You got any idea where Mason is now, Miss Starbuck?"

"He—or rather, his body—is at the mine, in the office. You see, Sheriff, after Jared killed Edmonds, he turned his gun on me. I had to kill him in self-defense."

"And you say you're Miss Starbuck? The one from Texas that owns the mines?"

"Yes." Jessie was not surprised at the sheriff's lack of surprise. She'd learned that most Western lawmen dealt with sudden death often enough to treat it almost casually. She went on, "If you need someone to identify me—"

"No, no, Miss Starbuck," Hicks said hastily. "Your word's good. Well, I guess you better set down and tell me about it."

Jessie made her story as brief as possible. Hicks listened, nodding occasionally. When she'd finished, he asked no questions but simply nodded again.

"Sounds like a pretty straightforward case to me," he said. "We'll have to make an investigation, of course, but with two witnesses, I don't see any problems. Is there anything else I can do for you now, Miss Starbuck?"

"No." Jessie breathed an inward sigh of relief. She'd been gambling that the Starbuck name would work its influence again, as it had for her so many times before. Then, as an afterthought, she said, "There is one favor I'll ask of you, Sheriff Hicks. If you happen to see my assistant in town, you could give him a message."

"I'd be glad to, except I wouldn't know him."

"Oh, you'd recognize him, I'm sure. His name is Ki. He's of Japanese ancestry."

Hicks asked, "You want me to go look for him?"

"I don't think that will be necessary, Sheriff. However, if you do see him, please ask him to return to the mine."

"I'll sure do that, Miss Starbuck. And anything else you need now, you come let me know."

"Thank you. I will. You've been very courteous and understanding, and I appreciate it."

Jessie turned to go, and had already gotten outside when a man behind her called out, "Miss Starbuck! Can I talk with you a minute?"

Turning, she saw one of the men who'd been talking in the corner of the sheriff's office.

"Of course," she replied, thinking he might have overheard her request to the sheriff to give Ki a message.

"I couldn't help overhearing what you told Dick Hicks," the stranger said. "My name's Timothy O'Grady. I'm the superintendent out at the Anaconda smelter, and since your mines are the only customer I've got outside of our own company, I think we'd better have a talk."

"I think you're right," Jessie agreed. "I had in mind calling at the Anaconda office before I went back to the mine, but running into you here will save me a trip."

"It didn't seem the right thing for me to break in while you were talking to Dick Hicks, but I'd sure like to know what's going to happen out at your mines, now that Jared's dead."

"I don't think this is the time or place to talk about that, Mr. O'Grady," Jessie replied. "Suppose we put off talking for a day or so, then we can—"

"Pardon me for interrupting, Miss Starbuck," O'Grady broke in, "but have you had lunch yet?"

"No." The question startled Jessie. Food hadn't entered her mind, but suddenly she realized how many busy hours had gone by since her breakfast.

"We have our own dining room at the smelter," he went on quickly. "You'll get a better meal there than you will at any of the restaurants in town, I'll guarantee that. If you have time, and will be my guest, we can have lunch together."

Remembering the meal she and Ki had eaten at the restaurant on the day they arrived, Jessie hesitated only a moment. "That seems an excellent idea, Mr. O'Grady. I'd be delighted."

"Good. It's quite a walk, unless you have a horse."

"I came in a buggy. It's in front of the building."

"Then I'll tie my horse to it, and we'll ride together."

As they started down the street that ended at the smelter, Jessie sized up her unexpected companion with quick sidewise flicks of her eyes. O'Grady had the open face, ruddy complexion, and blue eyes associated with the Irish, and under the rim of his derby hat she saw a fringe of neatly trimmed red hair. He was heavily built, though only two inches or so taller than she was. He was older than his boyish appearance indicated, she decided, somewhere just past thirty. It was a youthful age for him to have attained the position he held, under a demanding employer such as Marcus Daly was reputed to be.

O'Grady said, "I apologize for being—well, I guess overeager is about the most polite thing I can say, Miss Starbuck. But I'm concerned that with Jared Mason, uh, gone, there might be problems with the new superintendent."

"You shouldn't have any. I've already given the job to Mr. McKelway. I'm sure you know him."

"Oh sure. Mac's a nice fellow. A little old for the job, though, isn't he?"

"If I'd thought so, I would've hired someone else," Jessie replied a bit tartly.

"Now don't take me wrong, Miss Starbuck," O'Grady protested. "I didn't mean that as a snide remark. I was just thinking out loud."

"I see. Well, don't worry, Mr. O'Grady. We'll continue to send our ore to the Anaconda for smelting, unless Mr. Daly raises the price too much."

"I suppose I shouldn't ask you, but what would you do if he did that?"

"Build our own smelter at the mines, of course. It wouldn't be as big and imposing"—Jessie nodded toward the towering smokestack looming ahead of them—"but it would be as efficient as yours."

O'Grady looked at Jessie and smiled. His grin was so spontaneous and unaffected that Jessie found herself smiling too.

"I'll bet it just would," he said. "You know, you're quite some lady, Miss Starbuck."

"I suppose that's a compliment, so thank you, Mr. O'Grady."

"I meant it the nicest way possible," O'Grady said. "There aren't many women who've got the spunk to walk up to a sheriff and say what I heard you say back there."

"I didn't enjoy it, I assure you, but it had to be done."

"Oh, I can see that. But I admire you for it, just the same. Now if you'll just pull over to that hitch rail on the right, I'll tie up your nag and we'll go in and eat."

Jessie was not too surprised when she discovered that the smelter's private dining room had all the attributes of a private club for gentlemen. It was a large, quietly luxurious room, with silk drapes at the windows and linen-covered tables on a carpeted floor, the waiters immaculate in stiffly laundered white jackets. The food was also excellent.

She'd have expected nothing but the best from any enterprise in which Daly had a hand; he had a reputation as a demanding gourmet. Aided by the excellent food as well as by O'Grady's barely concealed admiration, Jessie and her host got past the prickly semi-antagonistic stage during lunch, and, by the middle of the meal, were chatting as friends.

She looked up in surprise after the soup course, when O'Grady asked her, "What about the man you mentioned to Dick Hicks? Ki, I think you called him."

"Ki was my father's friend and companion, and now he's mine," Jessie replied. "I've never known a more intelligent, loyal, and courageous man."

"Oh, I wasn't asking about his character," O'Grady said quickly. "I thought you said you came to town to find him."

Jessie nodded. "That's the only thing I have left to do. I was sure I'd see him, but so far I haven't."

"You know about the law here in Copperopolis that for-

145

bids anybody of Oriental birth to be on the street, I suppose?"

"I heard it mentioned the evening Ki and I got here, but I suppose it slipped out of my mind. Why?"

"Oh, I thought I might help you find him."

"I'd be very grateful if you would."

"Excuse me just a minute, then," O'Grady said. He left the table and disappeared into the swinging doors that led to the kitchen. When he returned, he slipped into his chair, nodded to Jessie, and said, "With any luck, your man Ki will be here by the time we finish our meal."

"How can you be so sure?"

"Orientals stay together, and since the smelter's not in Copperopolis, the town laws don't apply. We hire a few Orientals in the kitchen. I sent our Chinese salad chef out to their settlement to find him."

"But how could he hope to do that? Ki's a stranger here."

"He may be, but our man had heard about him. It seems your companion is quite a hero to the people in the settlement for having beaten up one of Saul Goodwin's chief plug-uglies not once, but twice."

"That would be the man they call Boston," Jessie said. She hesitated only momentarily before asking, "Have you heard much about Saul Goodwin?"

"Not as much as I expect to," O'Grady replied. "You seem to be the first target of his Knights of Labor."

"I suppose that's logical, Mr. O'Grady. From Goodwin's standpoint, we're much smaller than the Anaconda, so we should be easier to handle."

"After meeting you, I have a feeling Goodwin may be wrong. And could you bring yourself to call me Tim?"

"I was just about to suggest that we could be a bit less formal, Tim."

"Is it Jessie, then? Or Jessica?"

"Jessie suits me best."

"Fine. Now let's get back to Saul Goodwin, Jessie. Has he started bothering you yet?"

"So far there hasn't been any trouble, but I'm sure some of his enforcers are working in the mines. What's the situation here at the Anaconda?"

"About the same. Joe Fritch, the mine super, and I know we must have some, but they're not doing anything that we can see. Don't you think we should keep in touch with you, though, so we can compare notes?"

"Certainly, Tim. Ki and I came out here to clear up a problem that had been worrying me. I found that Jared Mason was the problem, so it's solved now. I'll be leaving soon, but I'll suggest to Mr. McKelway that he visit with you occasionally."

"I don't suppose you feel like talking about Mason?"

"No, I don't." They'd been eating while they talked, and had reached the coffee and dessert stage. Jessie pushed aside her dessert dish and added. "You wouldn't either, if there'd been a problem at the Anaconda."

"You're right, of course."

A waiter came up to the table, leaned over O'Grady, and whispered something to him. The smelter superintendent smiled at Jessie and said, "Ki is on his way here. You'll just have time to finish your coffee."

"You're a very efficient man, Tim. If you ever get tired of working here, let me know."

"I don't foresee any possibility that I'll be leaving, Jessie, but you'll be the first to know if I do."

True to O'Grady's prediction, Ki arrived just as they were finishing their coffee. Jessie saw him come in the dining room and started to get up.

"If you'd like for him to join us—" O'Grady began.

"No," she said firmly. "I must get back to the mines as

soon as I can. Ki and I will talk on the way. But thank you for lunch and even more for your help, Tim. I do appreciate it. We'll talk again before I leave."

Ki reached the table, and Jessie introduced him to O'Grady, then said, "We have a lot of ground to cover, Ki, and I'm sure Tim has work to do. We'd better go at once."

There were quick goodbyes, and Jessie and Ki went out to the hitch rail. As they got into the buggy, Ki said, "I didn't know you had friends at the Anaconda, Jessie."

"I didn't, until I met Tim O'Grady. But I was surprised to find him so friendly. They're keeping an eye on the Knights of Labor on the assumption that sooner or later they'll make trouble at the Anaconda."

"How did you happen to meet O'Grady?"

"He was at the sheriff's office when I went in."

"I hope you weren't there because you were arrested."

"No. I had to go in to report the murder."

"Murder!" Ki exclaimed, his almond eyes widening.

Again, Jessie found herself describing what had taken place after Ki left that morning. She concluded, "There's more to it than I've told you, Ki, but the rest can wait. I'm anxious to know what you've found out."

"Nothing at all, Jessie. But there's one person I haven't talked to yet."

"Belle LaTour?"

"Yes. I stayed away from her because I thought Mason might still be at her house, and I felt that you didn't want me to have a run-in with him."

"You were right, of course. But now that he's dead, your friend Belle should be willing to talk freely."

"I'd better see her at once. Saul Goodwin would like to take Mason's place. He was hinting at that the other night."

"I don't suppose you've seen Goodwin? Or the one called Boston?"

148

"Both of them seem to have dropped out of sight. I'd like very much to know where they are."

"Would you like for me to go with you to talk to Jared's light of love?" Jessie asked.

Ki thought for a moment, then shook his head. "No, I think she'd talk more freely if I was alone. Why don't you drop me off at her house? After I've spoken with her, I'll get my horse from the livery stable and join you at the mines."

"Yes, that's the best idea, I'm sure. I should be there to give Mr. McKelway and Eric confidence, anyway."

"Of course. And I'll join you as soon as I talk to Belle."

Chapter 14

Belle's eyes widened when she opened the door and saw Ki. "I didn't expect you, Ki," she said. "Come in before any of the neighbors see you. You know how jealous Jared is."

Ki realized there was no way he could soften the blow that Belle was about to receive. He said, "I'm afraid I've got some bad news for you, Belle. Jared Mason's dead."

For a moment Belle stared at him as though unable to grasp what he'd said. Then she asked, "How could he be, Ki? He was perfectly all right just a few hours ago, when he went to the Starbuck mines. Was there an accident?"

Ki saw that she was not going to dissolve in tears, but he tried to soften his news as much as possible. "He was in a gunfight, Belle. And I'm afraid that's all I can tell you."

"But what am I going to do now?"

"Do you have a family you can go home to?"

Belle shook her head. "No."

"How about money?"

"I've got some. Not a lot. Jared wasn't the kind to shave pennies, Ki. He gave me more than enough to keep the house up and buy food and clothes. And he gave me presents at first."

"What did you do before you met Jared?"

Belle was silent for several moments. At last she said, "I was a singer." Then, a bit defiantly, "I sang in saloons,

Ki. I wore tights and all like that. But I never was a—well, I never did take money from a man just to go to bed with him."

"I understand, Belle. But you know how to take care of yourself, I'm sure."

"You can just bet I do! I've done it before and I can do it again!" She was silent once more, then went on, "You've been real nice to me, Ki. Not like—well, like that Saul Goodwin."

"Has he bothered you?"

"Not lately. I haven't seen him since the other night, of course. But he's going to—" Belle paused thoughtfully, her brow wrinkled in concentration. "I guess I've got to get out of Copperopolis, Ki. If I don't, Goodwin will be after me, and he could make a lot of trouble for me."

"Why do you say that?"

"Because I heard him and Jared talking about what the Knights of Labor were going to do—how Goodwin's enforcers were going to ruin the Starbuck mine, get the men to go out on strike, and start fights to wreck the stopes and all."

"When is this supposed to happen? Do you know?"

Belle shook her head and said, "All I know is that they were going to start pretty soon."

"What else did you hear?"

"Well, Jared was going to be the big boss after Goodwin got the mine away from Jessie Starbuck. Then he was going to help Goodwin and his gang do the same thing at the Anaconda."

"But you don't know when they planned to move?"

"No. I do know something else, though." Belle paused, her eyes open wide in fear. "As soon as Goodwin finds out Jared's dead, he's going to remember all the things I heard them talking about, then he'll come after me. I think I'd better get out of here quick, Ki. Will you help me?"

"Of course I will. I think it's the best thing you can do. I'll go with you to the depot. The accommodation train will pull in from Virginia City in about three hours. Can you be ready to go by then?"

"Yes. I'm just going to pack my best clothes, and leave everything else the way it is."

"Start packing then. While you're busy here, I've got a job to take care of."

"You're not going to leave me by myself, are you?"

"Only for a few minutes. Belle, the other night you went out your back door to Goodwin's house. Is it directly behind this one?"

"Yes. Just go through the backyard. There's gates in both of the fences." Belle's face clouded as she went on, "Ki, you're likely to get in trouble if Goodwin sees you nosing around his house. He's real particular that way. I've got a special way to knock, so he knows it's me."

"Show me," Ki told her.

Belle rapped on the tabletop, two quick taps, then three more. Ki stepped up to her side and rapped as she'd done, copying the rhythm experimentally.

"What will you do if he's at home?" she asked.

"I haven't thought that far ahead. I'm betting he's not at home, though. Go pack now, Belle. I'll be back in a minute."

Ki stood on the back step of Belle's house for a moment, looking at the houses that faced the next street. No one was in sight. He went through the two yards to Goodwin's house and tapped out the rhythmic knock. He stood motionless, listening, for several moments, and when he heard no sounds of movement inside, he tried the door. It was locked, but he'd expected it to be. He looked at the back windows. They were covered by wooden shutters, the louvered panels closed and locked. Ki knocked again, and when he was sure the house was deserted, he turned and went back to Belle's.

"Did you find out anything?" she asked.

"No. Goodwin's gone, and I decided it was too dangerous to try to get in during daylight. If I could be sure I'd find anything when I got in, I might risk it, but not right now."

"Ki, what're you looking for?"

"I don't really know, Belle. I know that Goodwin and Jared Mason were trying to get Jessie Starbuck's mines away from her, and almost anything I can find out would help stop them. Did Mason have a place here where he kept papers of any sort?"

"No. Sometimes he'd bring letters from the mines to put in the post office, but he never left anything here."

Ki shrugged. "That was too much to hope for, anyhow. Are you almost through packing?"

"Yes. I've got my suitcase just about filled up, and laid out the clothes I'll wear on the train." Belle hesitated for a moment, then said, "Ki, you've been nicer to me than just about any man I ever met before. I owe you an awful lot, and all I can do is say thank you."

"You don't even have to say that, Belle. I don't expect anything, you know that."

"Will you do one more thing for me now?"

"Of course. What is it?"

"Just sit down on the sofa by me and put your arms around me and hold me till it's time to go to the depot. I don't mean—well, you know, I guess. I just want to feel like somebody cares something about me."

"Sure, Belle." Ki sat down and patted the sofa cushion. "Come on. We'll just sit here until it's time to leave."

Most of the afternoon had slipped away by the time Jessie reached the mine. She'd welcomed Ki's suggestion that he stay in town, for, as close as their companionship was, neither of them forgot for a moment that the primary responsibility for the Starbuck interests lay in Jessie's hands. She needed time to think about her next move, and very little thought was required to convince her that after the events of the morning she must move swiftly to make certain that the deaths of Mason and Edmonds would not affect the operation of the mines.

Her thoughts were interrupted twice. About halfway between Copperopolis and the mines, she passed the undertaker's wagon carrying the canvas-shrouded bodies of Edmonds and Mason. A few miles later, when she came within sight of Starhope, she drew up on the reins and brought the buggy to a stop while she stared with astonished interest. The little settlement was like a disturbed anthill. Its usually deserted streets were crowded with men and women, in pairs and trios and knots of a half-dozen, with people moving from one group to another.

Belatedly, Jessie realized that until the arrival of the undertaker, the night-shift miners and their wives had not known of the violent scene that had taken place in the office. She watched for a moment, then slapped the reins on the horse's back and drove the quarter-mile or less to the mine office. McKelway and Eric were sitting at their desks, ignoring the papers spread in front of them, and just staring at the walls.

Jessie decided at once that the best thing she could do was to ignore their shocked inactivity. She said briskly, "I'm glad you're both here, because we have some plans to make."

"We're ready whenever you are, Jessie," McKelway told her. "I don't think we've done much since you left—just tidied up a little bit, cleaned the floor over by the door, and straightened up generally."

"Of course, first things first." She drew up a chair between the desks at which the two men were sitting. As she settled into the chair, she said to McKelway, "You'll want to find a man to replace poor Mr. Edmonds as soon as possible, of course. I'm sure the two of you can handle the work until you do, but you'll both be busy getting acquainted with your new responsibilities."

"I don't mind working some extra time until we do, Miss Starbuck," Eric volunteered.

"I'll find someone soon enough to keep us from being overworked, Jessie," McKelway promised.

"Good. And you'll move into your office as soon as it's convenient, I'm sure. You and I will go over those reports and statements that were hidden in Jared's desk, and see how much work's going to be involved in getting things straight again."

"Oh, that won't be much of a job," McKelway said. "And if Eric has time, he can help with that."

"I have a special job I'm going to ask Eric to help me with this evening," Jessie went on. "I'm going into the mines to talk to the men. When I passed Starhope on the way here, it looked like every night-shift miner and his wife was in the streets, gossiping about what happened this morning."

A frown had formed on McKelway's face when Jessie announced her intention of going into the mines. He said, "I'm not sure that's a good idea. A mine's no place for a woman."

"I've been underground before," Jessie reminded him. "And that's the only place where I can get all the miners together at the same time, without interrupting their work too much."

"Yes, I can see that," McKelway agreed. "But don't you think I should go with you instead of Eric?"

"No. You've had a very bad day, and going down there

will be an extra strain that you shouldn't face."

"Now look here, Jessie, I'm not an invalid!"

"I don't think of you as one," Jessie assured him. "But how often did Jared go underground?"

"Not very often," McKelway said thoughtfully. "He kept his door open to them until just lately, but they came to the office, he didn't go to the mines."

"Exactly," Jessie said. "And until he went wrong, Jared was a very good superintendent."

"Yes, I'll give him that," McKelway agreed. "It's a shame the way he went bad."

"It's settled, then," Jessie told them. "I suppose the shift changes are still the same?"

"Still just like they always were," McKelway replied. "The day shift comes on at six in the morning and the night shift at six in the evening."

She turned to Eric and said, "I'd like for you to go find the day-shift boss and tell him to have the gang foremen bring all the men from Number Two and Number Three into the main drift of Number One. I'll only talk about ten minutes, but I don't want any of the men to lose by being there, so we'll give them all a half-hour's overtime pay to make up for what they'll lose by staying or by not being able to start digging at the regular time."

"I'll go right now, Miss Starbuck," Eric said.

"We still have over an hour," Jessie went on. "You'll probably want to put on dungarees, Eric, and I've got to change too, so let's meet here at five-thirty. I'm sure, from what I saw when I passed Starhope, that the gossip and rumors must be getting pretty wild by now, and I intend to do everything I can to settle things down immediately."

After she'd buttoned the fly of her jeans and shoved her feet into her boots, Jessie reached for her gunbelt. She pulled her hand back before she touched the holstered Colt, and shook her head, realizing that to wear a gun when she was going to talk to the miners would be a mistake.

Nothing in her appearance, she told herself, must give them the impression that she feared or distrusted them. She picked up her derringer and slid it into the invisible holster inside the leg of the left boot before putting on her jacket.

Eric was waiting for her. He had on dungarees, and his costume was topped off with one of the heavy padded caps worn by the miners, complete with a tiny carbide light attached to its peak in the front.

"Gee, you sure look nice, Miss Starbuck," Eric commented as she walked into the office. "You look more like a lady when you're wearing pants than you do without them."

Almost as one, Jessie and McKelway began laughing. When he realized what he'd said, Eric's face turned a fiery red. Jessie broke off her laughter to say, "Don't worry, Eric, I understood what you meant, and I'm not a bit offended. And if you don't mind, I'd like for you to call me Jessie."

"Oh, I couldn't do that!" he protested. Then he added, "But if it's all right with you, I'd like to call you Miss Jessie."

"I'll settle for that," Jessie replied. "Now, if you're ready, let's go. It's quite a walk to the mines, and we don't want to be late."

Men were walking in a steady stream along the railroad track toward the entrance to the valley. A long line of empty ore gondolas that extended from the valley entrance almost to Starhope stood on the track, waiting to be shunted into the valley. The cars kept the miners from walking along the railbed, and as Jessie and Eric fell into step beside them, there were some elbow-nudges and a few whispered remarks from those nearest. Finally a miner broke out of the line and came up to them.

"Ain't you Miss Jessie Starbuck, the lady that owns these here mines?" he asked.

"Yes, I am. Did you want to talk to me?" she said.

The man cleared his throat and began hesitantly, "Well, there's all sorts of yarns passing back and forth about what happened in the office this morning. I guess all of us has heard 'em, but we ain't sure we got the straight of it."

"That's why I'm going into the mine with you," Jessie said. "And I'd appreciate it if you'd ask your friends to pass along the word that I'm going to be there in the main drift of Number One and tell you about it myself."

"What about us that works in Two or Three? We'll be late getting to our stopes."

"You'll all be paid a half-hour's overtime for staying ten minutes to listen to what I've got to say," Jessie told him. "You might pass that word along too."

"You bet I will!" the miner replied. "It ain't often we get paid for not working!"

As word of Jessie's message spread along the line, the men began to talk among themselves, and many of them turned to stare at her and Eric with undisguised curiosity. They reached the mouth of the valley. A steady trickle of miners wearing dirt-stained dungarees was already coming out of the mouths of Number Two and Number Three and filing into the entrance of Number One.

They were joined now by the night-shift men arriving, and when Jessie and Eric went into the tunnel, it was packed as far back as they could see. Since most of the men coming off work had not extinguished their cap-lamps, the wide, low-ceilinged shaft was reasonably well lighted. The tunnel still held the smells that Jessie remembered, an acrid scent of raw earth, carbide fumes, and unwashed bodies.

"We'd better get down as near the center of the crowd as we can," Jessie told Eric. "Then perhaps all of them can hear me."

With Eric leading the way, they worked along the edge of the crowd, keeping close to the tunnel wall. They reached a point where one of the tunnel lamps was directly overhead, and Jessie tugged at Eric's sleeve.

"This is fine," she said, raising her voice above the babble of talk and laughter coming from the miners. "Now all I've got to do is get them to look at me and listen."

One of the miners standing nearby asked, "You want to get up high, where everybody can see you, ma'am?"

"It would be nice if I could," Jessie replied. "I didn't think to bring something to stand on."

"We'll fix that," the man said. He turned to the miner next to him and said, "C'mon, Ed. Make a cat's cradle with me for the little lady."

Facing each other and intertwining their hands, the two men stooped while Jessie stepped on the improvised platform. When they stood erect, her waist was at the level of the men's heads, and seeing her rise above the crowd, the miners standing closest grew quiet. Gradually the silence spread to the edge of the group, and Jessie started speaking.

"In case some of you don't know who I am," she said, raising her voice to reach those at the crowd's edge, "I'm Jessica Starbuck. My father started these mines, and built Starhope, and after he died I began trying to take his place.

"Now, all of you have heard that there was trouble in the main office today," she went on. "So you'll know the real truth about what happened, I want to tell you about it. Jared Mason had been embezzling, and we finally caught up with him. He pulled a gun and shot Fred Edmonds— all of you know who he was, because he handed out your pay envelopes every week. After Mason killed Mr. Edmonds, he turned to aim at me. I had a gun and shot him before he could kill me too."

A murmur rose from the miners. Jessie waited until it died down, then went on, "Mr. McKelway is the superintendent now. All of you know him, and you know he's a fair and honest man. What happened this morning isn't going to change a thing. The mines will keep operating, and Starhope will stay the same. My father tried to make the Starbuck mines a good place to work, and I've tried to run them the way he did. I want all you men to have a square deal and an honest wage and a decent place to live. I hope you'll keep on working here. That's all I have to say."

From somewhere at the edge of the crowd a voice called out, "What about the Knights of Labor?"

A murmur ran through the group and another man shouted, "We don't want the Knights of Labor! We got enough bosses telling us what to do!"

Another voice cried, "Shut up, you dirty scab!"

A few feet away from Jessie, some of the miners began trading punches. Others began trying to stop them. Within a few seconds the crowd became a seething, boiling mob.

Suddenly the men holding Jessie broke their grip to join the melee, and she dropped to the ground. She landed in a crouch, and was rising up to look for Eric when a sweat-stinking miner's jacket dropped over her head and a pair of muscular arms wrapped around her chest.

Blinded and clamped in a grip she could not break, Jessie tried to fight back. She kicked and squirmed, but her kicks met empty air and her struggle to break the embrace of her captor's brawny arms was useless.

★
Chapter 15

A voice close to Jessie's ear said, "Get her outta here fast, before things settle down!"

"Yeah," another voice replied. "Help me hide her while we get her to the hideout."

Bodies bumped Jessie's kicking legs as the man who was carrying her weaved along the edge of the crowd. Through the thick cloth of the padded dungaree jacket she could hear the shouts and curses of the fighting miners as she was carried along. She heard boards grating together, and the noise of the crowd suddenly diminished.

"Hand me that rope," the man holding her said. "We'll tie her up in my coat to keep her quiet till the boss gets here."

Rough hands wrapped a rope around Jessie below the arms of the man who still clasped her. Each time the rope encircled her, the loop was pulled so tight that it would have cut into Jessie's skin, but for the bulky coat swathing her head and torso. When the rope had been wrapped in closely spaced loops that extended from the middle of her upper arms to a few inches below her elbows, she felt it being knotted in the small of her back. The man who had been carrying her lowered her to the ground and released her.

"That'll hold her till Boston gets here," he said. "I don't know why the hell he told us to grab her, but I guess he must've had a reason."

"Maybe Goodwin told him to," the other man suggested. "We done what Boston said, anyhow, and that's all we need to worry about. Anything goes wrong, it's his ass, not ours."

Hearing the name of Goodwin's hulking enforcer caused Jessie's muscles to tighten. She remembered the derringer in the leg of her boot. Even blindfolded, she was an unusually accurate shot, for she had practiced shooting at targets that she located by sounds in the darkness. She strained to reach her boot top, but the ropes binding her arms were too tight.

"You think it's safe to leave her here by herself?" the first man asked.

"I don't see why not. Nobody but Boston and our bunch knows we're using the old stope, and the way we fixed it on the outside, it'll just look like another place where the drift had to be shored up."

"Well, Boston didn't tell us to stay, and she's tied up so tight there ain't no way she'll get loose. We might as well get up aboveground and breathe good air again."

Once again there was the scraping of boards that Jessie remembered hearing before. Then she was surrounded by silence. From the conversation she'd overheard, Jessie had already deduced that she must be in one of the abandoned stopes, its opening camouflaged to conceal the fact that it was being used by the Knights of Labor's enforcers. The packed dirt of the floor and the chill in the atmosphere confirmed her deduction.

After waiting a few moments to be sure the two men would not return, Jessie began working on her bonds. The rope had been wrapped cruelly tight, and her hands were already getting numb. In spite of its bulk and thickness, the jacket shrouding her head allowed air to filter through its fabric, and the strength of the muscles in her arms had not yet been affected. She concentrated on trying to spread her

162

elbows to stretch the rope, but the thick padding of the jacket that covered her head and torso kept her from exerting any force directly on the rope.

Soon Jessie became aware that her legs were getting cramped from their strained, straight-out position on the chill, moist ground. She was still sitting erect. She let herself fall back and rolled over on her face. The trained muscles of her body were not yet too cramped to respond. She brought herself up on her knees, then rose to her feet.

Disoriented as she was, standing brought on a wave of dizziness and she staggered a few steps, then her equilibrium was restored in spite of her inability to see. Since she was sure of the manner in which the enforcers entered and left the stope, she reasoned that if she could find the entryway, she might be able to push it open. She started walking, seeking a wall along which she could feel her way to the opening.

In her blindness, Jessie had lost not only her ability to judge distance accurately, but to walk in a straight line. She had been so eager to get started that she neglected to count the number of steps until she'd covered what seemed to be a very long distance. She stopped and started again. Though she had no idea how big the stope might be, she reasoned that twenty or at most thirty steps should take her to a wall.

After she'd counted twenty paces, Jessie kept moving in the same direction while she counted off ten more. When she still had not encountered a wall, she made a right-angle turn and started walking again. This time she'd covered only seven paces before she collided with the face of the stope.

She hit the vertical wall of raw earth so unexpectedly that the impact almost threw her to the ground again, but somehow she retained her balance. Keeping one hand on the wall, she began walking around the perimeter of the

163

manmade cavern, searching for the entrance.

Step by cautious step, Jessie followed the wall until her hand suddenly encountered rough wood. She ran her fingertips over the boards, feeling for a handle, covering as much area as she could with her arms bound. By now her arms were growing numb, and it seemed that an interminable amount of time went by before she felt a rough latch. Trying to picture its construction in her mind's eye, Jessie fingered the latch slowly. With success so close, she had to force herself to move deliberately, in spite of the urgency she now felt, to get out of the stope. She finally felt the hinge pin, and the L-shaped iron strap into which the latchboard dropped.

Sliding her fingertips under the board, she began lifting it slowly and carefully. She'd almost freed the board from its retaining L when it flew from her hands and the door was pushed open with a scraping of wood. The door opened inward, and Jessie had no time to step away from it. The rough door crashed into her, and she fell to the ground.

"Well now, just look-a-here!" Boston's heavy, harsh voice grated. "Damn near got away, didn't you? Lucky I showed up, or you'd of been long gone!"

Instinctively Jessie opened her mouth to reply, but her common sense took over in time, and she said nothing. Big hands closed around her waist as Boston lifted her to her feet. Then the hands were pawing her. When the rope around her body kept him from fondling her breasts, he brought his hands down and ran them over her body to her hips, and down her flat stomach to rub her crotch and stroke her taut buttocks.

"Damned if you don't feel firm and smooth all over!" Boston said. "You might not like what you got coming, but I sure will! I been wantin' the worst kinda way to put it to you ever since I seen you that night in the restaurant, and I got plenty of time to do it now. It'll be an hour or two before the boss gets here, and I ain't gonna waste a minute of it!"

Jessie held her body rigid as the big man continued to paw her. She racked her brain for a way to attack him, but without her arms and hands to balance her movements, even the kicking attacks that she'd rehearsed so often with Ki were of no use to her.

"Don't start figuring how you can get away," Boston went on gloatingly. "I ain't gonna take a chance and untie you, just pull your pants down and bend you over and give it to you dog-style. But after the boss finishes with you and hands you back to me, I'll have lots of time to try some other ways."

Jessie stifled the anger that flooded her, and clenched her teeth as she felt the big man's hand feeling for the buttons of her jeans.

"If I were you, I wouldn't stay in Virginia City," Ki told Belle as they stood on the depot platform, waiting for the accommodation train from the south. "The mainline train should be waiting when the accommodation gets back to Virginia City. Just step off and get right on that mainline train and go on to Bozeman or Billings, or even beyond."

"It sounds like you think Saul Goodwin's going to be after me, Ki," Belle said, a worried frown puckering her brow.

"I don't think he is yet," Ki replied. "But if he sees you, he might decide you know too much about him, and then you'd be in danger. And Virginia City's fairly close."

"I'll do what you say, then," Belle replied. "But I sure wish you were coming with me."

Before Ki could reply, a train whistle sounded, and in a few more moments the locomotive came into sight as it rounded the bend beyond the station. As the train drew closer, Ki took Belle's arm and led her to the rear of the crowd of passengers who'd been drawn from the depot by the whistle.

"We'll try to be inconspicuous," he said. "As soon as the train's unloaded and the passengers start boarding, you get in the middle of them. They'll shield you while you're crossing the platform to the train."

As the engine drew closer to the depot, it showed no signs of slowing down. When it reached a point where the cars behind it were visible, Ki saw that behind the locomotive and tender there were only two cars. Then another locomotive whistled as it came into sight around the bend.

"That first train must be a special of some kind," Ki said. "It's not long enough to be the regular accommodation. That's the one just coming around the bend."

Its speed only slightly diminished, the first train swept by the depot platform. Ki saw that the first car was a baggage car, the second a day coach. As the two cars flashed past, he saw the conductor standing in the vestibule between the baggage car and the coach. Behind the conductor, Ki got a flashing glimpse of a man peering out, scanning the platform.

Brief as Ki's look was, he recognized Saul Goodwin. Through the coach windows he saw that its seats were occupied by a score of men, rough types wearing dungarees. Then the coach had passed the depot and begun to pick up speed as it rolled on.

Ki's reaction was immediate. He said to Belle, "Goodwin was on that train, Belle. You don't have to worry about him any longer. You'll have to get on the train alone, but you don't need me to help you now."

"But why?" she asked. "Ki, what's happening?"

"There are only two places that train could be taking Goodwin and his enforcers. One is the Anaconda, the other is the Starbuck mines," Ki explained, speaking rapidly. "The way Goodwin and Jared Mason were working in cahoots, I'm sure he's taking a bunch of his enforcers from Virginia City out to attack Jessie's mines. I've got to go, Belle. Good luck."

Before Belle could ask any more questions, Ki was hurrying away from the depot. He started running toward the livery stable as he dropped off the platform, but a voice from the hitch rail stopped him. He turned and saw Tim O'Grady untying his horse.

"I'm sure you saw who was on that special train," O'Grady said as Ki paused.

"Yes. I'm heading for the mines right now."

"Where's your horse?" O'Grady asked.

"At the livery stable."

"If you'd like company, I'll ride out with you," O'Grady offered. "I know some shortcuts across country that might get us there ahead of the train."

"I'll be more than glad to have you," Ki replied. "Start riding. I'll catch up with you."

Boston's thick fingers found the buttons they were seeking. Jessie put up the only defense she could think of, twisting and squirming. Boston wrapped his free arm around her chest to hold her still. Supported by his arm, Jessie could now use her feet. She lashed back in an upward kick, and Boston grunted angrily when her boot heel landed on his shin.

Jessie had a target now, and she struck with lightening speed. As soon as the foot with which she'd kicked Boston's shin hit the ground, she brought up her other foot. This time she aimed higher and put more force into the kick, and Boston yowled with pain when the heel of her boot struck his testicles.

He released his hugging arms as he doubled up, his hands grasping his crotch. Jessie fell forward to the ground and began crawling away from him, propelling herself with her feet, the thick jacket shielding her head as she scuttled across the dirt floor. She could not see where she was going, but that did not matter. She only wanted to put space between herself and Boston.

Jessie had covered only a few yards in her awkward retreat when she heard Boston's footsteps thudding in pursuit. She rolled on her back and lashed out with her feet, but being blinded by the jacket defeated her. Boston's ham-like hands grabbed one flailing foot, then the other. Twist and struggle as she might, Jessie could not pull free.

"Damned if you ain't the toughest bitch I ever did tangle with!" the big man growled. "But I got you now, and this time you ain't getting away!"

Held immobile, Jessie could do nothing. With a sinking sensation, Jessie felt him tugging at her left boot—the one with the hideaway derringer holstered inside. It was on the verge of slipping off her foot when she heard the familiar sound of wood rasping on wood that told her the door was opening again.

"Boston!" a man called urgently.

"Get the hell outta here!" Boston snapped. "I'm busy!"

"You got to come right now!" the man said. Jessie recognized his voice; he was one of her original captors. He went on, "She can't get away, and we need help bad! Our boys are getting whipped by these damn Starbuck miners!"

"All right!" Boston replied. Jessie felt the pressure of his hands leave her ankles. He said, "I'll come back and take care of you in a minute, you sneaky bitch! And you ain't gonna get away, next time!"

Jessie heard the grating sound of the door opening and closing. She lay limp, regaining her strength, but the noise

168

of the door brought her alert and tense again within moments. Then she relaxed as she heard a familiar and welcome voice.

"Miss Jessie!" Eric said. "Hold on a minute while I get my knife out." She sensed the youth's presence as he knelt beside her and began sawing on the rope that bound her. He went on, "I figured you must be in here when I saw that big fellow come in, but there were too many out in the tunnel for me to do anything."

Suddenly the pressure of the loops on her arms and torso was released. Jessie felt Eric's hands lifting her shoulders, and sat up while he unwound the rope. He whisked the jacket off her head and she blinked for a moment, her eyes watering. Even the glow of the carbide lamp on his helmet seemed blindingly bright.

"Thank you, Eric!" she said, looking through slitted eyelids at him, then at the dirt walls of the stope. "I don't think I've ever been as glad to see anyone as I am to see you."

"We've got to get out of here," Eric said, helping Jessie to her feet. "There's fights going on all along the tunnel. Our men are whipping the enforcers, though."

"Then we'll let them finish the job," she said. "We'd better get back to the office. Mr. McKelway's there alone, and they may be attacking it too."

Emerging from the stope into the main drift, she saw that the struggle had become one of small individual groups instead of a single massive brawl. The miners were so busy with their fights that she and Eric had no trouble dodging around the four or five knots of struggling, fist-swinging men and reaching the tunnel's mouth. The valley was deserted in the low-slanting afternoon sun. They hurried to its opening and trotted along the line of gondolas on the tracks until they could see the office building. It stood peacefully deserted, and they began running toward it.

McKelway opened the door and stepped out on the narrow porch to greet them. He looked at Jessie's dirt-stained jeans and disheveled hair and asked, "Jessie, are you hurt? What happened? You look like you were in an accident of some kind."

"I'm all right," Jessie told him. "But there's a riot in Number One. My guess is that the Knights of Labor thought Jared's death gave them a good excuse to try to wreck the mines."

"They may attack the office," Eric added. "We'd better get ready to stand them off."

"But I don't under—" McKelway began.

Jessie broke in, "We can talk later. I'm going upstairs to get my Colt. You and Eric get the rifles and shotguns ready. As Eric just said, they might be here anytime."

Ki and Tim O'Grady left Copperopolis at a gallop. As they drew away from the town, O'Grady left the road. He slowed his horse as they began riding cross-country. Ki let the Anaconda man take the lead, following him as he cut through the low underbrush, dodging between the small young second-growth cedars and pines. As their horses slowed while mounting a long steep slope, O'Grady motioned for Ki to come abreast, and Ki spurred up to ride beside him.

"We'll beat Goodwin's train there, unless we have trouble with the horses," O'Grady called to him. "The railroad makes a big loop to avoid the worst grades. What I've started wondering now is what we can do when we get there!"

"Let's get there first," Ki said, "and see how much of a lead we've got on them."

O'Grady motioned toward the skirts of Ki's saddle. "Too bad we haven't got rifles. I've got a pistol, and I hope you have one."

"I haven't, but don't worry," Ki replied. "I'll hold up

my end in a fight. How did you happen to be at the depot? I got the impression that you expected to see Goodwin and his thugs."

"I did. At the smelter we've got a private telegraph line to Marcus Daly's office in Virginia City. Our men down there have been watching Goodwin for quite a while. They wired me he was bringing a bunch of men up here, and warned me that the smelter might be in danger."

They reached the crest of the slope, and O'Grady pointed to a string of smoke-puffs off to one side. The puffs were dissipating in the bright late-afternoon sunshine. Ki gauged the distance between their present position and the smoke that marked the location of the train. He judged it to be about three miles.

"We'll beat them by maybe ten minutes," O'Grady said.

Ki nodded, then told O'Grady, "Ten minutes will be plenty, if we handle things right."

O'Grady stared at Ki, a startled look on his face. Then he toed his horse into a gallop again, and Ki followed suit. They plunged ahead, gaining speed, as they rode across the downslope.

Chapter 16

Their horses winded and lathered, Ki and O'Grady pulled up at the railroad tracks across from the mine office. They looked back along the railroad tracks, but the train was not yet in sight. Reining their horses around, they rode up to the office door and dismounted. They were wrapping the reins around the hitch rail when Jessie came out on the porch.

She stared in surprise at O'Grady, but before greeting him, she turned to Ki and said, "You got here just in time. Goodwin's enforcers started a riot in Number One, and for all I know they're still fighting in there."

"That explains a lot," Ki told her. "But the fight in the mine will have to wait." Without any further explanation, he turned toward the railroad tracks and started studying the long line of gondolas.

Seeing Jessie's bewilderment, O'Grady explained, "Goodwin is on the way here himself, Jessie, with a day coach full of his men." Then he added, "I hope you've got rifles in your office."

"But how—" Jessie stopped short and shook her head. "I guess explanations can wait. How close is the train?"

"It'll be here in about five or ten minutes," Ki replied as he turned back from looking at the tracks.

"How many men are with him?" Jessie asked.

"We don't know," Ki replied. "Tim and I just got a quick look at the train when it passed the Copperopolis station.

We saw Goodwin, but didn't have time to count his enforcers."

"My guess is that there are at least fifteen or twenty," O'Grady volunteered. "What about rifles, Jessie?"

"We've got two. And two shotguns. I've got my Colt, and Mr. McKelway and Eric both have pistols."

"Ki?" O'Grady asked.

"I have my own weapons," Ki replied. "Not guns. I must be close to a target to use them." Without explaining further, he turned to Jessie and went on, "You and Tim stay here, Jessie. You'll know when to use the rifles."

"What are you planning, Ki?" Jessie asked.

"Those gondolas will give me perfect cover," Ki told her. "The train will have to stop when it gets to them. I'll hide in the first car and attack when the enforcers start walking along the tracks to the mines. I'll use *shuriken.*"

O'Grady looked bewildered, but Jessie nodded as she grasped Ki's plan with the speed that came from their long companionship in fighting the cartel's forces.

"We'll hold our fire until they're disorganized," she said.

"Will you please tell me what you two are talking about?" O'Grady asked. "I don't see how Ki—"

"You'll see later, Tim," Jessie promised. She turned back to Ki. "Get in place. Tim and I will handle things here."

As Ki started off at a trot toward the tracks, the puffing of the approaching train could be heard. Jessie told O'Grady, "We need to check on ammunition, Tim. Let's get inside before the train gets close enough for Goodwin and his men to see us."

Ki reached the first gondola in the string and swung himself up by the catch-bar. He vaulted over the side of the car, noting that the two-inch-thick boards of which it was made were thick enough to stop a bullet. When he stood on the floor inside the open-topped car, the sides reached

173

to his chest. Down the tracks, the locomotive of the train carrying Goodwin and his enforcers came into sight. Ki hunkered down and waited.

As they went into the office, Jessie asked Tim, "I suppose you're a good shot with a rifle?"

"Good enough, at the range we'll be shooting," he said. "I don't see—"

"You will," she repeated as McKelway and Eric came up to them. They'd taken the rifles from the rack behind the door, and Jessie told them, "Let Tim and me use the rifles. You take the shotguns and use them if Goodwin and his gang get too close."

"Goodwin?" McKelway frowned. "Where is he, Jessie?"

"On a train coming from Copperopolis, with some of his enforcers."

"But what about the mines, Miss Jessie?" Eric asked.

"They can wait," she replied. "It's more important for us to keep this new bunch of enforcers from getting to the mines."

"I'd feel better if I knew what you and Ki were planning, Jessie," O'Grady said. "What in the devil can he do by himself, against fifteen or twenty men armed with rifles and pistols?"

"Don't worry about Ki," Jessie told him. "His *shuriken* are all he needs at first. Then he'll use *ninjutsu.*"

"I don't know any more than I did before," O'Grady told her with a puzzled frown. "But there's no time to explain now. Listen!"

They heard the puffing of the locomotive and the grating of its steel brake shoes on the wheels as the engineer brought the two-car train to a stop. They rushed to the windows and saw Goodwin swing to the ground from the day coach. He waved to the men inside to follow him, and they started along the track to the baggage car. Goodwin crawled inside the car, and, in a moment, returned to the door with two rifles. He handed them to the first men in the line along the tracks and disappeared again.

O'Grady threw open the office door and brought up his rifle. Jessie stepped to his side and pushed the gun's muzzle down. He said, "Now's the time to hit them, Jessie! Before Goodwin can get those rifles handed out!"

"Wait, Tim," Jessie told him. "Give Ki a chance."

Crouched in the ore gondola, Ki remained motionless until he heard the crunching of booted feet on the loose stone ballast as the enforcers got off the train. When the sounds of moving men faded to the occasional sound of shuffling feet, he risked peering quickly over the edge of the gondola. Beyond the locomotive he saw Goodwin handing rifles to his plug-uglies and decided there was no reason to delay his attack.

Ki took a stack of *shuriken* from one of the many pockets of his black leather vest. Although he could throw with equal skill using either hand, Ki's position in the corner of the gondola limited him now to right-hand throws. Holding the thin stack of blades in his left hand, Ki slipped the topmost one off into his right hand.

When he raised his head above the side of the gondola again, Ki saw that the two men who'd just received their rifles had stepped off the ballast to the sloping grade. They stood facing away from him. With a quick flick of his right hand, Ki sent the first *shuriken* whirling to its target. Before it had landed, the second blade was on its way.

Ki had chosen the most vulnerable exposed spots of the two enforcers as his targets—the area at the base of each man's neck where sensitive nerves and the main branch of the big artery from the aorta lay just below the skin, protected only by a thin layer of muscle. The two *shuriken* reached their targets within seconds of each other. The first, then the second of the enforcers gave a gurgling cry of pain and both men dropped their rifles as they clawed at their throats.

In the instant after he'd sent the second *shuriken* spinning toward its target, Ki dropped below the gondola's side. He heard the cries of pain and the shouts of the men waiting beside the baggage car when they saw their companions staggering, blood spurting from their throats, hands clawing at the shining blades. With a third *shuriken* in his right hand, and his left hand ready to slide a fourth from the stack, Ki stood up again.

Gathered around the two men who'd been hit with Ki's first throws, the enforcers did not see him. Quickly picking his targets with trained skill, Ki launched the next two *shuriken* and dropped below the car's side without being seen. The fresh outcries from the crowd of enforcers told him that he'd hit his marks again.

Goodwin's voice rose above the angry shouts that were now coming from the enforcers. "Scatter, you damn fools!" he commanded. "You're sitting ducks, bunched up the way you are!"

"Hand out the rest of them guns!" one of the men yelled.

"Where in hell did them things come from?" another shouted.

Booted feet were scrabbling on the railbed now as Goodwin's men scattered, trying to find cover. The engineer and fireman leaped out of the locomotive cab and started running along the right-of-way toward the mines. Bending double, Ki ran to the opposite side of the gondola. He vaulted over it, landing on his feet, the steel-spring muscles of his legs absorbing the shock as he hit the railbed. He ran back to the special train, its locomotive hiding him until he got to the tender.

With one quick leap he grasped the top rim of the tender's

side and snaked over it. Belly-wriggling across the water tank, Ki peered down. The enforcers had drawn revolvers now, and were still scattering in response to Goodwin's command. Some had started forward beside the locomotive, while others were fanning out down the sloped embankment toward the road.

Ki launched a *shuriken* to his left, its target one of the men trotting toward the rear of the train. While it was still spinning in midair, he loosed a second blade on a closer mark, an enforcer who was moving along beside the locomotive. As soon as he'd freed the second *shuriken*, Ki leaped to the top of the baggage car and flattened himself out, *ninja*-fashion, on the side of the walkway opposite the road.

"There's two of 'em out there!" Goodwin shouted from the shelter of the baggage car as the men at opposite ends of the short train fell, clutching at their throats. "Split up, damn it! Half of you go each way!"

"You come out and show us!" one of the plug-uglies yelled angrily. "We still ain't seen nobody!"

"Look on top of the cars!" Goodwin ordered.

Hearing feet scraping on the crawl-bars that led to the top of the baggage car, Ki rolled off without hesitation. He landed on his feet, but the long drop tested even his well-trained muscles, and he was slow in springing up after the jarring impact. The enforcer who'd reached the top of the baggage car saw Ki as he sprinted for the underbrush on the slope beside the right-of-way.

Ki heard the man's shout and changed his course to a zigzag. Even so, the slugs from the enforcer's revolver kicked up spurts of dust uncomfortably close to him as he dove into the cover of the brush and snaked along on his belly parallel to the train. Behind him, bullets splatted into the spot where he'd entered the brush. Ki stopped and lay quietly for a moment, listening to the shouts rising from the surviving enforcers as they circled the train and converged on the slope.

In the office, Jessie and her companions watched the enforcers floundering in confusion under the impact of Ki's surprise attack. They were too far away to see the momentary flashes of the *shuriken* or to hear Goodwin's orders and the shouts of his plug-uglies, and only Jessie's trained eyes caught an occasional glimpse of Ki as he moved around.

"I don't know what Ki's doing, or how he's doing it," O'Grady said, as they saw the enforcers circling the train to get to the underbrush on the slope where Ki had taken cover, "but he's sure cutting them to ribbons."

"There'll be plenty of time for explanations later," Jessie told him. Knowing what to expect, she'd seen the almost invisible movement in the brush as Ki escaped on the slope. "But it's time for us to give him a hand. The odds are on our side now." She said to McKelway, "You and Eric stay here with the shotguns to cover us if we have to retreat. Tim? Are you with me?"

"I can't think of anybody I'd rather be with!" he replied.

At a dead run they started across the road. As they reached the train, Jessie said, "We'll take cover in the coach, and hit Goodwin's men from behind."

"What about Ki?" O'Grady asked. "He's on that slope somewhere. We don't want to risk hitting him."

"If I know Ki, he'll be under the coach before we get there, or inside it," Jessie said. "Or in one of those gondolas."

O'Grady shook his head, his face showing his incredulity. He gaped when they got inside the day coach and saw Ki entering through the rear door.

Ki wasted no words. He said to Jessie, "They're ready to panic. You potshoot from here. I'll go back to the gondola. I've still got a few *shuriken*."

Breaking the glass from the coach windows with the muzzles of their weapons, Jessie and Tim O'Grady began peppering the slope. The already disorganized enforcers were thrown into utter confusion when one, then another fell to shots fired by Jessie and Tim as they began their unexpected attack from behind.

Some of them turned and made a halfhearted rush to counterattack the coach, but when Ki brought down the man closest to him with a spinning *shuriken* from his position in the gondola, the fear of their invisible attacker took the fight out of the others. The enforcers turned and began running along the tracks toward Copperopolis.

With a sigh of relief, Jessie laid her rifle down. She walked to the rear of the coach and looked out at the straggling line of the retreating enforcers, then said, "I'm glad it's over without any of us getting hurt. I was—" She broke off as a noise from the front of the coach drew her attention. Turning, she saw Saul Goodwin standing in the aisle, a revolver in his hand covering her and Tim.

"It's not over yet!" Goodwin snarled, swinging the pistol from Jessie to Tim as he spoke. "You've ruined the best setup I ever had, damn you! But you're not going to be around to ruin the next one!"

Jessie dropped to the floor, drawing her Colt as she went down. Her shot was a split second later than Goodwin's, but the slug from the Colt took Goodwin in the heart while his bullet buzzed over Jessie's head. She heard Tim grunt as Goodwin crumpled to the floor of the coach, and got to her feet quickly. Tim's left arm dangled at his side. He held his right hand clamped to his upper arm, blood oozing between his fingers.

"Are you hurt badly, Tim?" Jessie asked.

"I don't think so. It burns like hell, but I don't think it's too serious."

Jessie unbuttoned his shirtsleeve and pushed it up his

arm to the point where his hand stopped it. She whipped off the bandanna she'd been wearing around her neck.

"Let go now," she told him. "I'll get this tied over it, and we'll put on a real bandage when we get back to the office."

Tim took his hand off the wound and looked at it curiously while Jessie wiped away the blood. He said, "This is the first time I've ever been shot. Funny, but it doesn't hurt much."

"It will later," Jessie said, wrapping the bandanna around the shallow crease cut by the bullet. "But you were lucky. The bullet just grazed you."

Ki came into the coach. He looked at Goodwin's body, then at Jessie and Tim, and said, "I don't understand how I missed seeing him when I looked in the baggage car. He must have been hiding behind the boxes of dynamite."

"Dynamite?" Jessie asked, her eyebrows rising.

Ki nodded. "A half-dozen cases. He was planning to blow up the mines, Jessie. It's lucky Tim and I spotted him back in Copperopolis and got here as fast as we did."

"We're not through with his enforcers yet, though," Jessie reminded Ki. "They may still be fighting at the mine."

"You stay here and put a better bandage on Tim's arm," Ki said. "I'll go with McKelway and Eric and see what's happening at the mine."

Letting McKelway set the pace, they walked down the road to the valley mouth. Little knots of men stood around the opening of the main tunnel leading into Number One. As they drew closer, they could see that a number of the men in each group had their hands bound behind their backs.

"It looks as if the miners have taken care of the enforcers," Ki commented.

"Yes," McKelway agreed. "I think the Starbuck men have won the battle."

They were within a few dozen paces of the tunnel mouth when another group of prisoners was ushered out into the valley. Ki saw Boston among them. It would have been impossible to miss seeing him, for the big man towered above the men around him. Boston saw Ki at the same time. He gave an angry roar and, with a twist of his bulging arms, snapped the ropes that secured his wrists. Brushing aside the miners around him, the giant started toward Ki.

Ki did not hesitate. He ran to meet Boston. In the few seconds that elapsed before they came together, Boston's rage-twisted face warned Ki that he must finish their fight quickly and with finality, for he faced a battle to the death.

Ki waited until Boston's hamlike outstretched hands were almost near enough to close on him, then he struck. Springing high and swinging his body as he rose in a *tobi-geri* kick, Ki landed the bone-hard point at the front of his foot, between the instep and big toe, on Boston's temple.

Ki's blow was a crushing one, as he had intended it to be. The giant's relatively thin temporal bone shattered like thin porcelain, driving sharp shards into Boston's brain. Boston stood erect for a moment, swaying, his eyes rolling upward. Then his knees collapsed and he folded to a heap on the ground.

When Boston did not stir, McKelway came up and stopped beside Ki. Astonishment in his voice, the old man said, "I think you killed him, Ki."

"Yes. He was Saul Goodwin's chief helper. He had to die to assure that you would have peace here again."

After Ki and the others had gone, Jessie looked around the office and shrugged. She said, "There's nothing here that I can use for a bandage, Tim. Come on, we'll go up to the apartment. There are towels and some clean dish cloths there, and I have a bottle of permanganate in my suitcase.

You wouldn't want your arm to start festering."

"It's just a scratch, Jessie!" Tim protested. "I can get a doctor to bandage it when I go back to town."

"No. Let's fix it now," Jessie insisted. "Come on."

In the apartment, Jessie led Tim to the small kitchen and ran water from the cistern tap into a tin dishpan. She told Tim, "You'll have to take your shirt off. Will you need some help?"

"No. I can do it all right."

He started unbuttoning his shirt while Jessie got the permanganate from her suitcase. She mixed a few grains with the water she'd drawn. She took a clean dish towel from the cabinet and tore several strips from it before wetting an edge of the remainder and squeezing it above the bandanna to soften the kerchief and the blood that had clotted under it.

While she worked with quick efficiency, Jessie glanced now and then at Tim. He'd taken his shirt off, revealing a triangle of light brown hair curling on his chest. The muscles of his arms flexed under his smooth skin as he moved them while trying to see the wound.

After a moment he gave up and watched Jessie while she completed her preparations. He said, "You're doing this as though you've had a lot of experience taking care of gunshot wounds."

"More than I like to think of," she replied. "Now move over here and stand still while I take off the old bandage."

Holding Tim's biceps just above the elbow, Jessie pulled off the bandanna. She felt his biceps tighten, but he did not try to jerk his arm away, and said nothing to indicate that he'd felt anything. A trickle of blood started from the livid gash. Jessie mopped the blood away, soaked a corner of the cloth with the antiseptic, and patted it on the raw flesh.

"Hold your arm out and bend your elbow," Jessie said.

"And keep it steady while I put on this fresh bandage."

Tim extended his arm and bent it as Jessie had told him to, but when she began to put on the bandage, the arm kept getting in her way.

"This isn't going to work," she said. "Lean on the table, and I'll move over in front of you."

Bracing his backside against the table, Tim extended his arm again and Jessie stepped in front of him. He brought his forearm back, and when she turned to begin wrapping the bandage, its corded muscles brushed against her breasts. She felt her nipples begin budding in response to the soft pressure, but kept on wrapping the bandage neatly until the wound was covered.

Ripping off the excess cloth, Jessie leaned forward to tear the end into strips that could be tied around Tim's arm. As she turned while tying the knot, her hip pushed into Tim's groin, and when she felt the pressure of firm flesh, she realized that he had an erection. She said nothing, for the stimulation of the danger they'd shared and conquered together was working on her senses, too. She tied the knot and started to step back.

Tim took Jessie's arm and held her pressed against him. He said, "I've wondered about you from the first minute I saw you."

"Wondered what?"

"Whether you're a real woman or one who just teases a man."

"Why don't you find out?" Jessie suggested.

Tim pulled her to him. Jessie turned unresistingly, and when he bent to kiss her, she raised her lips to meet his. Their tongues met and twined, and Jessie felt his erection swell and grow as he pulled her against him more firmly. They broke the kiss and their glances met. Jessie read the question in Tim's bright blue eyes.

"Now, of course," she told him. Her hands went to his belt and she freed the buckle. Keeping her glance locked on his, she added, "We don't have much time, but there'll be other times later, before I leave."

She leaned back against the table and he dropped to his knees in front of her and removed her boots as she undid the buttons of her fly. Then he slid the close-fitting denims down her long legs and off, and dropped them to the floor. When he stood again, she opened his fly and released his jutting shaft. She turned her mouth up to him for another kiss, and while their tongues probed each other's mouths, she slid his rigid manhood into place and, with a quick thrust of her hips, brought him fully into her. He grasped her buttocks with both hands, and she raised her feet from the floor and wrapped her legs around his back, locking her ankles together. Their bodies remained interlocked as they stood this way for a few moments. Then Jessie lay back on the table to allow Tim greater freedom of movement. He began to drive in long, slow thrusts, withdrawing almost completely, then plunging into her again. Jessie began to quiver and moan as his thrusting increased in tempo.

She did not even try to exert her control. She was as anxious as Tim was to reach their peak. They were seized at almost the same time. Jessie's orgasm mounted rapidly to its dizzying height, and Tim cried out with a long, sobbing groan of delight. They clung together while he flowed into her, and sighed together when their bodies grew quiet, and they clung together in quiet exhaustion.

"What do you think now?" Jessie whispered to Tim when she could find breath enough to speak.

"I think you're the most woman I've ever known, Jessie," he replied. "Come back to town with me tonight, please do!"

184

"I can't, Tim. But tomorrow's another night, and there'll be one after that, and still others later. I'm not going back to Texas right away. For once, I'm in no hurry to return to the Circle Star."

Watch for

LONE STAR AND THE MOUNTAIN MAN

twenty-fifth novel in the exciting LONE STAR
series from Jove

coming in September!